Jady

"Please come back to work, Grady,"
Clarice asked in her nicest voice.

He knelt down to fiddle with something on the tamale stand. "Sorry."

"I'll give you a raise."

"He looked over his shoulder at her. "If you go out with me Sunday—"

"You're not serious!"

"Oh yes I am."

"Since when does a man with a bod—" She felt she was on fire. What was the matter with her, anyway? Then out came his slow grin.

"With my what?" he asked, eyes twinkling.

"Have to blackmail someone into going out on a date?"

"With my what?"

"You know what!" she snapped.

He came closer to her then, and she backed up a step into the trunk of the oak tree. He tilted her chin, and she knew he was going to kiss her. And she wanted him to, more than she'd wanted anything in a long time.

"Go out with me Sunday night," he said.

"If you'll come back to work at the restaurant," she insisted.

He smiled. "Now why would someone resort to blackmail who has a bod—"

"Grady!" she said, a warning in her voice. But he moved too quickly for her to resist the lips that captured her own. . . .

P9-CAJ-801

WHAT ARE *LOVESWEPT* ROMANCES?

They are stories of true romance and touching emotion. We believe those two very important ingredients are constants in our highly sensual and very believable stories in the *LOVESWEPT* line. Our goal is to give you, the reader, stories of consistently high quality that may sometimes make you laugh, sometimes make you cry, but are always fresh and creative and contain many delightful surprises within their pages.

Most romance fans read an enormous number of books. Those they truly love, they keep. Others may be traded with friends and soon forgotten. We hope that each *LOVESWEPT* romance will be a treasure—a "keeper." We will always try to publish

LOVE STORIES YOU'LL NEVER FORGET
BY AUTHORS YOU'LL ALWAYS REMEMBER

The Editors

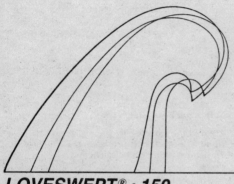

LOVESWEPT® • 150
Sara Orwig
Hot Tamales

 BANTAM BOOKS
TORONTO • NEW YORK • LONDON • SYDNEY • AUCKLAND

HOT TAMALES

A Bantam Book / July 1986

LOVESWEPT[R] *and the wave device are registered trademarks of Bantam Books, Inc. Registered in U.S. Patent and Trademark Office and elsewhere.*

Cover art by Enric.

All rights reserved.
Copyright © 1986 by Sara Orwig.
Cover art copyright © 1986 by Bantam Books, Inc.
This book may not be reproduced in whole or in part, by mimeograph or any other means, without permission.
For information address: Bantam Books, Inc.

ISBN 0-553-21767-4

Published simultaneously in the United States and Canada

Bantam Books are published by Bantam Books, Inc. Its trademark, consisting of the words "Bantam Books" and the portrayal of a rooster, is Registered in U.S. Patent and Trademark Office and in other countries. Marca Registrada. Bantam Books, Inc., 666 Fifth Avenue, New York, New York 10103.

PRINTED IN THE UNITED STATES OF AMERICA

O   0 9 8 7 6 5 4 3 2 1

One

I won't look! Clarice Jenkins told herself as she turned the corner on Apache Avenue, gazing down the wide street. Cars passed her in the next lane, heading in the opposite direction. The summer sun was bright, with a clear blue sky above Oklahoma City, Oklahoma. But Clarice's life wasn't quite so sunny.

She gritted her teeth, then clamped her jaws shut, staring straight ahead of her so intently her eyes stung. "I won't look. I'll drive right past and never glance that way! Never!" *Think of something,* she told herself feverishly. She'd count to ten in Spanish and that would help her ignore it. *It.* She made a growling sound deep in her throat as the image of it came to mind. *It!* She hated, loathed, and detested it! And couldn't keep her eyes off it! *It* was making her life miserable, because she kept looking, no matter how hard she tried not to.

"Nrrrr." She made another deep-throated sound as she approached the drive to King's Crown, the restaurant where she worked. She thought of how life used to be when she turned onto Apache Avenue. In the good old days, before the last two weeks, her spirits would lift and she would be invigorated, filled with enthusiasm over King's Crown, the restaurant that belonged to Uncle Stanton and had been temporarily placed in her hands, as well as Uncle Theo's and her younger brother, Kent's, for safekeeping.

But that had changed. Her peace of mind was gone, her temper was short, and the drive along Apache Avenue was fraught with turmoil and aggravation.

"Uno, dos, tres," She would stare straight ahead! *"Cuatro, cinco, seis."* She slowed as she approached the drive to King's Crown. She wouldn't look. *"Siete, ocho, nueve, diez."* Her counting became faster, the words running together as she felt the compulsion pull with the force of gravity, a tug of nature that all the will-power in the world couldn't resist.

Her senses drawn inexorably, she stiffened to fight the urge with all her might. She stared at gray concrete without blinking until she realized she had shot past the driveway to the restaurant!

She glanced in the rearview mirror, braked, and began to back up. Fortunately no cars were coming at the moment. She felt her cheeks grow hot to match her temper. She had passed her own drive-way! Out of the corner of her eye she could see a col-orful blur that made her want to gnash her teeth, yet at the same time steadily drew her attention with the pull of a freight engine.

"Uno, dos, tres, seis, siete— Darn it!" She looked.

There *it* was in full majesty—The Chest. A broad, bare chest, skin as burnished as teak and muscled to perfection, with short dark hair sprinkled over

it. The Chest held her attention with the steadfast-
ness of Krazy Glue. How she wanted to ignore that
chest, its owner, and his ghastly business, but
every time she passed she couldn't help but glance
at him. Her gaze swept upward, and her rage
reached mega proportions because he was
grinning at her!

His big Mexican sombrero was tilted to the back
of his head, its fringe of multicolored balls dancing
with each movement of his head. His chest was
vulgarly bare, his slim hips covered in frayed,
faded cutoffs, and he was laughing at her for
passing her own driveway! Beside him was the
revolting tamale stand—the dinky, tacky little hot
tamale stand that detracted from the dignity and
class of King's Crown. The ultimate touch of tacki-
ness was the fluttering, gigantic banner that read,
"O'Toole's Hot Tamales, Yum-Yum!" It was canted
at an angle, the paper banner stretched between
two poles he removed each night and set up each
morning.

He waved; she didn't. She lifted her chin, nodded
coolly, and swept into the drive.

She glanced at the oaks to her right. Grady
O'Toole owned a triangular strip of land next to the
land owned by Uncle Stanton. It was Grady's land
and it was zoned for business. He had cleared
enough room at the front for two or three cars to
turn in and park to get tamales beneath the shade
of a tall, spreading oak.

As she followed the curving graveled drive,
Clarice felt the tenseness go out of her shoulders,
but not her aggravation. It was twofold: first, she
was enraged that of all the patches of ground in the
city, Grady O'Toole insisted on setting up his

sleazy business right next to something as stately and beautiful as King's Crown. And second, she wished with all her being that she could drive past Grady O'Toole and not be compelled to look at his body!

Her gaze swept across the sloping lawn that ran to the charming Cape Cod–style restaurant, and she began to calm a fraction. The east side of Uncle Stanton's property was bordered by the O'Toole land, but to the north and west was a city park. Just west of the restaurant was a small lake with graceful swans, a sight that until two weeks ago had never failed to soothe Clarice's nerves.

Uncle Theo had talked to Grady O'Toole and had exhausted any possibility of getting the tamale stand moved agreeably. Now Uncle Stanton was searching for a legal loophole to get rid of O'Toole. Actually, Clarice had secretly agreed with Uncle Stanton's judgment that Uncle Theo had been the wrong person to send to run someone off—Uncle Theo had as much assertiveness in him as a daisy.

She stared at the lake, praying that Uncle Theo, Uncle Stanton, and the attorney could find some way to get Grady O'Toole to push his hot tamale stand to another location.

The gravel drive forked. One branch ran in front of the canopied entrance to the restaurant, and the other branch circled the building to the back, where it widened into a parking area for employees. Clarice stopped in the shade of a tall sycamore, by the big blue dumpster that held the restaurant's trash, and hurried inside.

The day had started badly with her embarrassment in passing her own driveway and facing Mr.

Grady O'Toole's grinning countenance. As she opened the back door the day grew worse.

"Help! Help!"

Cries reached her, and she recognized the voice of her brother, Kent. She ran down the narrow hallway toward the kitchen and saw Uncle Theo coming from the front, a towel thrown over his shoulders. He reminded her of an overgrown cherub, with his full pink cheeks and big blue eyes, and his mop of unruly brown curls that were beginning to show streaks of gray. She reached the kitchen first and raced inside to find her brother dangling from the circular brass light fixture. Kent's shock of blond hair tumbled over his forehead, almost hiding his blue eyes. His long jean-covered legs flayed the air and muscles bulged in his thin arms as he clutched the brass chandelier. A ladder lay on the floor and Clarice righted it quickly.

"Kent, good heavens! What happened?"

He locked his legs around the ladder, straightened, and stood on it while Clarice held it to keep it steady.

"I was cleaning the light fixture, and the ladder fell out from under me," he said.

"Mercy!" Uncle Theo said. "Be careful. Let me hold the ladder." He looked at Clarice. "Don't you look pretty today in your blue dress! Mr. Vickers is coming at lunchtime, and I want you to meet him."

"Uncle Theo, don't match-make! You don't need to introduce me to our male customers," Clarice said with a laugh.

His blue eyes twinkled. "I know I don't need to, but Mr. Vickers is a nice man."

She couldn't resist and leaned over to kiss his cheek. "You're sweet."

He beamed with pleasure as he said, "I talked with Mr. O'Toole this morning. Perhaps, Clarice, if you talked to him, you could get him to move his stand."

"What did he say to you?"

"He said he would give it some thought."

"That's what you told me he said yesterday and the day before."

"That's why I think you should try to reason with him. Maybe just a little additional prodding." Uncle Theo's eyes—as blue as her own—became round while he gazed at her solemnly. She had a peculiar feeling that he wasn't telling her everything.

"I don't know," she said. "I think I'll leave Mr. Grady O'Toole up to you."

"Hmmm. Stanton called this morning and said he thought the health inspectors would be out this week and to have everything spotless. I'm working on the front room, and Kent's cleaning the kitchen."

"I'll be here in the kitchen, getting food ready for lunch." She glanced at the big clock that hung on the wall above the gleaming stainless steel sinks. "We'll have to stop cleaning at ten when Cuong gets here and starts his cooking."

She put her purse in the tiny cubicle she used as an office, next door to the padlocked room that was Uncle Stanton's office.

The time went swiftly as she worked. Uncle Theo bustled behind the bar, mixing drinks. She seated customers, checked on the kitchen to see that things ran smoothly, and supervised the waitresses while Kent bused tables. When she had time Clarice also cooked, trying to follow Chef Cuong Nguyen's orders.

After the lunch rush, they cleaned while Cuong prepared dishes for the evening crowd. Uncle Theo and Kent worked on the large main dining room, with its white-linen-covered tables and vases of fresh roses on each table beside blue candles. During the afternoon two new paintings arrived. While Clarice stood in the center of the room watching Uncle Theo get ready to hang one of the paintings, she looked around the restaurant. Sunlight poured through the two large bay windows in front. Green plants were suspended from the ceilings and sat on the windowsills, giving a freshness to the room. The walls were paneled and tastefully decorated with oil paintings and antique clocks. The west wall was glass, giving a full view of the park and lake as well as the graceful willows at the edge of the water. To the east was the long narrow room that served as a bar, with small tables and upholstered chairs.

As she admired the new paintings, one a seascape and the other a five-masted schooner at sea, she heard a sudden spate of Vietnamese. Chef Nguyen was a taciturn man, seldom given to words, yet now, surprisingly, words poured from him. No translation was needed to make Clarice understand that something dreadful had happened.

Kent came running from the kitchen, the swinging doors flapping behind him.

"Sis, come look! We can't get out the back door."

"What are you talking about, Kent? I came

through the door this morning, and it worked fine."

"It's buried in dirt."

She gave him a disbelieving look.

"No, honest," he said. "There's dirt way up to the roof."

"There can't be," Clarice said. "I'll go see." Uncle Theo put down his hammer and scratched his head thoughtfully, waiting for her to lead the way.

She hurried through the kitchen to the back hall. Chef Nguyen waved his arms at her as he passed her on his way back to the kitchen. She didn't understand what he was saying, and she barely heard him because her attention was on the door at the end of the hall. Or where the door had been. It stood open, and dirt filled the doorway, a mound spilling into the hallway.

"What on earth?" She moved closer.

"Watch out, Sis. More could come in and cover you up."

The words were no sooner said when clods began falling from the top of the doorway, streaming down on her. She started to run, when she realized there was a person at the top of the door. She saw tufts of brown hair. More clods fell and she stared up into a dusty face and sea-green eyes.

Another spate of dirt showered over her as white teeth flashed in a grin. And she knew that grin. It belonged to The Chest. Her temper surged forth with the force of gale winds.

"You! What's the idea of this?"

"Sis, you better move back," Kent said from somewhere behind her. Clarice barely heard because of the roaring in her ears. She was trembling with fury, and this time she did give in to the urge to shake her fist at the grinning face at the top of the mound of dirt.

"You lowlife tamale aborigine!"

His grin widened, a figurative red cape flashing in front of her. She took a step forward. "What do you think you're do—"

Suddenly he yelled, and dirt began pouring through the door. She screeched and turned to run as a mound of dirt showered over her and something hard, solid, and heavy knocked her to the floor.

The breath went out of her lungs and she saw brightly colored stars, then blackness. She coughed, blinked, took in a deep breath, and choked on dirt. She couldn't move. Fright turned her to ice. She was buried beneath a mountain of dirt. She tried to wriggle away—and with a shock realized instantly she wasn't buried under dirt. She was under *The Chest*!

She felt the length of long legs tangled with hers, a solid weight covering her, the warmth of The Chest, that same bare chest she had stared at every day for the past two weeks. And now she was mashed beneath it. She wriggled again, then stopped swiftly. She blushed from her collarbone to her temple, deciding that if she smothered to death, she would lie still and not wriggle her derriere one more wriggle against that very male body. Then his weight rolled away and he sat up, pulling her up.

"Are you all right?" he asked. His big green eyes peered at her, thickly lashed bedroom eyes that made her forget the circumstances and her aching ribs and knees. Tasting dirt, she remembered, and moved away from him as she tried to stand up.

"Ouch!" she yelped, and started to fall as pain shot through her left ankle. Strong arms went around her, and he caught her, coming up on his feet with a swiftness that was remarkable. And she was staring straight ahead at his bare chest, about one inch away. All the dirt in the doorway couldn't hide the appeal of that broad chest. It was dusty, and slightly covered with sweat, but the muscles were obvious, the shape magnificent. She sagged and leaned forward, momentarily unable to resist pressing against him any more than she could resist looking at him when she drove past.

The Chest felt as marvelous as it looked. Her wits returned and she squirmed away, keeping her weight on the uninjured foot and bracing herself against the wall.

"Want me to call a doctor?" he asked. He looked truly concerned, but Clarice told herself it wasn't going to do him any good. Magnificent chest or no, she would keep her mind on the mountain of dirt.

"I want to call the police! Look what you've done!" She waved her hand at the pile of dirt.

"I'm sorry, but I'm getting it out of here. And I can explain—"

"You've blocked our only back exit! If the fire marshalls find out, they can close us down."

"I'm not trying to close you down," he said calmly, and suddenly she had a suspicion he was beginning to laugh at her. A muscle twitched in his cheek and his eyes had a sparkle, making her temper jump upward another notch.

"Dammit!" she said.

"Whoo-woo!" Kent exclaimed from the kitchen doorway while Grady O'Toole pursed his lips.

"How soon will you have it removed?" she asked.

"I'm shoveling it out—"

"Shoveling! That'll take a week to remove! How'd it get here in the first place?"

"As I started to say, I bought a truckload of dirt to fill in a low spot, where my hot tamale cart stands. When it rains, my cart stands in water. I left to run an errand after the noon crowd—"

"Ha, the noon crowd!" she couldn't help but exclaim. "Your two customers who come at twelve?"

He grinned. "Yep. My—er—*two* customers. As I was saying when I was interrupted, I left to run an errand and stuck a note of instructions on my tamale cart for the delivery men to dump the dirt in back. They must have misunderstood and thought I meant in back of this place."

"How could they misunderstand?" she asked with narrowed eyes. "And anyone ought to have sense enough not to dump a truckload of dirt against the back door!"

"You'll have to ask them," he said, and held out his hand. "We haven't met. I'm Grady O'Toole."

She would just as soon have taken hold of a hot iron as grasp his big, dirty hand, but she was too polite to refuse. Warm fingers closed around hers in a firm grip, and she looked up into laughing eyes that carried an invitation to join the fun. His face was smudged with dirt, except for his mouth. His full underlip and faintly curved upper lip held another kind of invitation. The laughter in his eyes changed, and his brows rose as a questioning look came over his features.

"Hello," Uncle Theo said pleasantly. Clarice jumped, dropping Grady O'Toole's hand instantly.

"Hello, sir. Sorry about the dirt. This was a

mistake. I was gone when they delivered it and I can't imagine why they dumped it at the door, but I'm shoveling it away from here as fast as I can."

Uncle Theo blinked, looking startled. "You're shoveling it? Can't they come back with their truck and scoop it up?"

"I can't get them right now. I'll keep at it until I get a path cleared."

"A path won't do," Clarice said firmly.

"Give the man time," Uncle Theo said. "Mr. O'Toole, this is my nephew, Kent Jenkins. This is Mr. O'Toole, who owns the tamale stand."

While they shook hands the phone rang, and Kent left to answer it in the kitchen.

Clarice returned to the subject, placing her hands on her hips. "You can't just clear a path—you have to remove every last clod of it! We can't close the back door now."

"I'll get the dirt out of your hall. If you hadn't opened the door, it wouldn't have come pouring in," he said quietly, adding to her anger.

"Sis, Uncle Stanton wants to talk to you," Kent said.

"Just a minute," she said to Grady, and stepped around the corner into the kitchen, walking carefully on her aching left foot. She picked up the receiver of the wall phone and lowered her voice, but Grady O'Toole was only a few yards away in the hall, and she suspected he could easily hear every word.

"Clarice!" Uncle Stanton snapped, and she could imagine his frown, his black eyes glaring at the phone and his handlebar mustache quivering.

"Yes, sir," she answered while she rubbed her ankle. It was beginning to feel better.

"I want to see you at my room at nine o'clock tonight," he said in clipped tones.

"They won't let me into the hospital then. It's past visiting hours."

"Stuff and nonsense. They damned well will. You're my blood kin and I have a right to have my family visit me. Nine o'clock you be here, d'you hear?"

"Yes, sir," she said in resignation, not wanting to have an argument. "I'll be there."

"Kent said you did a good noon business."

"Yes, sir."

"Bring me the register receipts."

"Yes, sir."

The phone clicked in her ear and she stepped back into the hall. Uncle Theo was heading toward the dining room. Kent passed her as he went to work in the kitchen.

Grady O'Toole was facing the mound of dirt, but looked down when she joined him. "How's your foot?"

"It's better. I'll be all right."

"I'm sorry this happened."

"I don't really think you are," she said coolly. "I don't see how a mix-up could have been made when it concerns an entire truckload of dirt! I think you did it on purpose!"

"Do you now?"

Her temper began its usual trek when his eyes started to sparkle with amusement. "Why do you think I'd dump a big truckload of dirt at your back door?" he asked.

"To foul up our business. To retaliate because we're trying to get rid of you. How would I know what warped reason you tamale types would come up with? Any big, healthy man who stands around half naked all day with a tamale pushcart has a way of life I don't understand!"

He pursed his lips and studied her, making her uneasy. "Half naked? My bare chest bothers you?"

Suddenly she wished she never had brought up the subject. "You better get to shoveling."

"Well, I'll be damned. My chest does bother you! Is that why you drove straight past your driveway this morning?"

"Darn it!" she exclaimed, feeling her cheeks burn and hating the big, slow grin that was appearing on his pesky face. "No, my thoughts were on business."

"Sure, they were! You're not married, are you, Clarice?"

"It's absolutely none of your business!"

"My, my. Things are looking brighter."

"They may be looking brighter to you, but they're not to me! We have three employees who come to work at four, another at five, two who leave at seven—and now they'll all have to come and go through the front. I'm not pleased to have them coming and going where people are trying to dine quietly."

"Sorry, but can't your employees walk quietly through to the kitchen or do they sing and dance their way in?"

"You think this whole thing's funny, don't you?"

He leaned closer to her, putting his hands on his hips. She wanted to back up, but there was a wall of dirt behind her.

"Miss Jenkins," he drawled, "you're wound up tighter than a toy on Christmas morning!"

She couldn't get her breath. The temperature in

the hallway had jumped to a tropic heat. He glanced over his shoulder, then looked back at her with a gleam in his eye that declared his intention as clearly as the "O'Toole's Hot Tamales, Yum-Yum!" sign over his cart.

"Don't you do it!" she said breathlessly, her heart pounding.

He blinked suddenly, and a look she couldn't read came over his features. The tension between them was broken and he stepped back, dropping his hands to his sides.

She knew he had started to kiss her. And he had stopped when she warned him not to. The twinkle came right back to his eyes.

"Don't I do what?" he asked.

She raged inwardly, amazed how one human being who was probably six feet six inches, almost two hundred pounds, maybe over, could be thoroughly infuriating. "Whatever you were about to do," she said with as much dignity as possible and with the most peculiar feeling deep inside—one she didn't want to explore.

"I was about to kiss you, and you know it!" he said, and laughed.

"Why don't you get back to shoveling dirt?"

"This is more fun," he said with jolly good nature that didn't calm her ruffled feathers at all.

"I'm sure it is! You don't like work, do you, Mr. O'Toole?"

He grinned and shrugged. "I'd say talking to a pretty lady is better than shoveling dirt any day!"

"But that dirt has to be removed!"

"Yes, ma'am. I'll work on it right now. And I didn't have it dumped here to cause you trouble. I'm not at war with my neighbors."

Her temper lowered a notch. He was beginning to sound pleasant and human. And she was having a difficult time keeping her gaze from lowering again, drifting down over The Chest that was only a few feet away. One thing she'd learned—dirt didn't detract one iota from its appeal.

He took a step closer and she wished she had moved away when she had the chance. She was once again hemmed in by walls, dirt, and Mr. Grady O'Toole. "You have a brother—surely you've seen bare chests before."

She had never known a person who could have the effect on her temper that Grady O'Toole could. Up her temper soared, and she fought the stupid urge her eyes had to lower and look at the subject of the conversation.

"Don't puff up your ego. Your chest is neither here nor there," she said with what she hoped was icy dignity. Meanwhile a little inner voice was screaming that his chest was *there* and *here*—a gorgeous chest that took her breath away every time she viewed it and was all too close to her right now.

"Is that so?" he said. "Why are you avoiding looking at me—the half-naked part of me, that is?"

"I'm not!" she shot out, taking a good long look at his chest. Too late, she realized she had just committed a major error in dealing dispassionately with Grady O'Toole. She couldn't view his chest without reacting to it. Her mouth went dry, her breasts tightened, and her cheeks grew hot. And for a moment she wondered what it would feel like to trail her fingers across his solid warmth, to be pressed against hard muscles. . . .

"Take all the time you want," he drawled in the

deepest, most sensual tone of voice she had ever heard in her life. Her knees lost their function, her senses reeled, and she ached to touch him. She blinked, trying to remember where she was and who he was. *The Chest.* The best-looking male chest in the next five dozen counties, and she had to confront it.

She took a deep breath and looked up to see his smile. Dazed, she smiled in return, then remembered what she was doing.

"If you'll get to work, I can get to work," she said.

"This is more fun," he said softly.

"Mr. O—"

"C'mon, Clarice, call me Grady. Never Mr. O'Toole. Friends shouldn't be so formal."

"We're not—"

"We're gonna be," he said, and sent her pulse galloping. "Now, I'll shovel dirt. You just go right on looking at my chest all you want," he said solemnly, and she shook with pent-up fury.

But she controlled herself and even managed to smile. The last thing she wanted to do was let Grady O'Toole know he bothered her. "Thanks, Grady," she said, and sailed past him into the kitchen, forgetting her sore ankle completely.

Grady O'Toole turned to watch Clarice Jenkins's blue skirt switch against her legs. Judging from the way the skirt clung, she had long, shapely legs. *Stop flirting with her,* he told himself. He didn't have time for a woman to complicate his life right now. And a woman like Clarice wasn't his type. She was as old-fashioned as Christmas and straitlaced to boot. But she had the biggest blue eyes and the clearest skin, and a walk that made him stop and stare.

Grady, you're working too hard, he told himself as he clambered over the dirt to get his shovel. He had to agree with Clarice. Anyone should have sense enough not to dump dirt at a doorway.

Grimly he began shoveling, and the vision of Clarice stammering about his chest drifted into his mental view. He chuckled. She was old-fashioned all right. Her walk wasn't, the little inner voice of his libido said, and he shoveled faster. *Forget her,* he told himself. That kind of woman was pure trouble. Look at her—he didn't know her and already she wanted to get a shirt on him! Think about . . .

He threw aside a shovelful of black dirt and paused, realizing there wasn't anyone to think about. Since his breakup with Peggy, there hadn't been anyone else except an occasional date. He was too busy with his life.

"Mr. O'Toole! Will you please get to shoveling!"

He turned around to see Clarice standing in the doorway, frowning at him.

"Right-o," he said with more good nature than he felt. She was getting on his nerves, he thought. A busybody, prissy, prim, with lips waiting to be kissed. . . .

He scooped up dirt, but instead of the black clods he saw her parted lips, the blue vein in her throat that had throbbed wildly, the flutter of her eyelashes. She had wanted him to kiss her. And he almost had before reason told him what a foolhardy act it would be. Women like Clarice Jenkins were trouble. Big, blue-eyed Trouble.

Look at him now. He couldn't do something as simple as shovel dirt for thinking about her. He gritted his teeth and worked furiously, feeling the sweat pop out on his arms and forehead. At dinnertime he stopped, washed up, and went out to sell tamales for two hours while sleek cars whipped down the drive to the King's Crown entrance, where a valet opened the doors for customers and parked their cars.

Finally Grady closed his tamale stand and returned to shoveling. As the sun slowly set, he shoveled the black dirt, dumping it on top of the Oklahoma red clay at the front of his lot, gradually clearing a path from the door of King's Crown and lowering the mounds of dirt on either side. Tomorrow he would get the delivery people out to finish the job. Night came, but the lights around the restaurant illuminated the parking area and the drive, and it wasn't difficult to see.

As he wheeled loads of dirt down the drive and returned with the empty wheelbarrow, he could see Clarice moving around the restaurant, seating customers, overseeing problems, helping in the kitchen. He tried to keep his mind on dirt and off her blue eyes, but it was a losing battle. His shoulders and back began to ache, and he yanked the empty wheelbarrow off the drive and gave it a shove, wondering how he had gone so swiftly from president of his own drilling company to a tamale vendor shoveling dirt!

He decided he needed several things immediately: dinner, because his stomach was protesting; a bath, because he was covered in dirt; and a date with a beautiful, exciting, sophisticated woman who thought he was charming, because he needed to forget Clarice Jenkins. He needed a date with someone who would not call him a tamale type!

He locked up the stand and moved it deep on his

lot, chaining it to a tree. For a moment he stared at it, thinking about his cousin Bart, and O'Toole Drilling. He glanced at King's Crown and shrugged before he walked to his black Lincoln and climbed in, enjoying the comfort of the big car. There was no road, only a beaten path where he had been driving in and out the past two weeks. At that moment the back door to King's Crown opened and yellow light spilled across the mounds of dirt. Clarice was framed in the doorway and his pulse jumped—a jump that made him firm his lips and remember his resolution to get a date with some-one beautiful tonight. Madeline, Patsy, Rita? He mulled over the possibilities while he sat with the car engine idling. He watched Clarice Jenkins cross the lot to her small, battered red Ford, noticing that she favored slightly the injured ankle and remembering how it felt to have the soft length of her stretched beneath him, what the wriggle of her derriere had done to him. She started her car, turned onto the drive, and disappeared down the street.

He drove slowly to the street, his mind blank, his shoulders aching from a mountain of dirt.

Clarice turned east, heading toward the hospital where Uncle Stanton was recuperating from foot surgery. She found him propped in bed, studying a restaurant magazine. His brown hair was a tangle, and rimless glasses were perched on the end of his nose.

He looked up when she came in.

" 'Evening, Uncle Stanton."

"It's nigh on to late night. Did you come straight from work?"

"Yes, sir," she said as she sat down in a brown vinyl chair and crossed her legs. She placed some papers on the edge of his bed. "How are you feeling?"

"Tolerable. How was business?"

"Here are the receipts and we had a very good night."

"Hmm. What's this I hear about dirt in the hall?"

Clarice frowned, wondering how Uncle Stanton had heard about it so quickly. "It was Mr. O'Toole, who has the tamale stand. He ordered dirt and the delivery men thought it was for us."

"Dumb place to dump dirt! Now, what I want you to do tomorrow, Clarice, is take an offer to the O'Toole man. I want him away from my restaurant! Here's a list of three small plots of land—bigger than what he has and just as good a location. If he'll move, I'll sell whichever one he wants, buy his land for the same amount, and give him a thousand-dollar bonus. To a man with a tamale stand a thousand dollars should be a great incentive."

"You don't know this man," Clarice said, wishing she didn't know him either. In addition to all the other pesky things about him, he stayed in her thoughts like peanut butter on her teeth. She didn't want to think about him; she didn't want to deal with him.

"What's different about him?" Uncle Stanton asked, giving her his full attention.

"He's annoying. It's a little hard to explain." She wasn't about to talk about her reaction to The Chest.

"Hell's bells. There must be something more specific."

She floundered, racking her brain for a way to convey what a dilemma Grady O'Toole was. "He's one of those people who could stand still on a traffic island and have every car in the city stalled in minutes. Things happen around him—like dirt blocking our back door. He didn't do it, he didn't know about, but it's his fault indirectly that it happened. Why don't you just wait for him to go broke and move on to another job?"

She could all but see the wheels working in Uncle Stanton's brain. She waited, knowing he'd snap at her to keep quiet if she tried to talk.

"Dammit, I don't want to wait," he finally said. "It detracts from our classy appearance for a tamale stand to be parked right beside our entrance. The man has to have his price. And in the tamale-stand business, the price shouldn't be too high. I'll tell you what, Clarice, offer him two thousand to make the exchange."

"I'll tell Uncle Theo, and he—"

"No!" Uncle Stanton thundered. "The most businesslike person working at King's Crown is you. You make the offer."

"Thank you—"

"Don't flatter yourself! If my toes weren't so damned pestiferous . . ." He turned to fix narrowed dark eyes on her.

"I want you to make the offer to O'Toole tomorrow. I want that damned tamale stand away from my restaurant! I have one of the most elegant restaurants in the city and one of the most beautiful settings for it. I'm not going to have it loused up by a rinky-dink, two-bit tamale vendor. He can just peddle his tamales elsewhere! And you see to it he does."

"I'll do my best."

"Tell him if that dirt isn't gone by ten o'clock tomorrow morning—"

"I won't see him until after ten in the morning," she interrupted.

"You don't go to work until after ten?"

"I do. Sometimes Mr. O'Toole doesn't. There isn't much demand for tamales for breakfast."

"Tell him the dirt has to be gone by noon or we sue. And by Jerry Crickets, I will!"

"Yes, sir," Clarice answered glumly. She didn't want to deal with Grady O'Toole.

To her relief a dump truck had come early the next morning. The dirt had been scooped up and moved to Grady's property. As Clarice worked, preparing the restaurant for lunch, she developed an uncustomary clumsiness, dropping things, bumping into furniture as she glanced continuously next door. Finally she saw the familiar black car pull onto the lot and stop in the shade of a tree.

Grady stepped out, and sunshine splashed over his bronzed chest. The muscles in his back rippled as he leaned down to pick something up from inside the car. The faded cutoffs molded trim hips, and muscles tightened in his long legs. When he turned around Clarice's mouth felt dry, and she couldn't resist letting her gaze drift slowly down to Grady's Top-Siders, then back up to The Chest.

She didn't want to deal with Grady, and momentarily was torn between going against Uncle Stanton's orders and tangling with Grady O'Toole. She watched as Grady unchained his white tamale cart and pulled it down toward the curb.

Firming her jaw, feeling as if she were about to step into a lion's den, she told Kent she was going to see Grady O'Toole.

She stopped in her office to pick up the paper Uncle Stanton had prepared with the list of properties he would sell to Grady. She stepped into the ladies room to look at herself in the wide mirror. Oklahoma City was sweltering in a heat wave. Although King's Crown was cool, it was hot in the kitchen, so she had dressed as coolly as possible in a pink sundress with spaghetti straps.

After smoothing hair that was neatly looped and pinned on top of her head, she went next door.

Two

He didn't see her coming at first. He stood with his back to her, working on the tamales, a spiral of steam rising from the stand. The big Mexican hat was tilted forward over his head, the little colored balls hanging from the upturned brim dancing as he moved. She had to admit, Grady O'Toole had the best physique she had ever seen. He should have dumped the tamales and gone into modeling.

She thought about Rick, whom she had been dating off and on for the past six months. Rick had a marvelous body and a pleasant personality, but there were no sparks. Regretfully she was coming to the conclusion that Rick was growing as bored with her as she was with him. Sparks. She stared at the broad bare shoulders that glistened with beads of perspiration. There were sparks when she was around Grady O'Toole all right, she thought. And how she hated every little one of them! She didn't want her chemistry to react to a man who stood around half naked, cooking tamales and wearing a ridiculous hat. And the banner that ran above the property—"O'Toole's Hot Tamales, Yum-

Yum!" That would be enough to send Uncle Stanton straight back to the hospital.

She stepped carefully, avoiding twigs, because she wanted to postpone the encounter until the last possible second. Grady was more than half naked, she mused. And the vision of how he would look without the faded cutoffs floated into her mind as insidiously as the drifting odor of tamales cooking—a clear image of his trim buttocks, long, muscled legs, a back that made her grow hot . . .

She blinked, clamped her jaw closed so tightly it hurt, and tried to think of something else. She forced her thoughts to the safety of weather. It was a lovely day, although growing hot already. A deep blue summer sky was dotted with dazzling white clouds, and the faintest breeze kept the air from becoming sticky. It was still early enough in the morning to be fairly pleasant, and in the shade of tall oaks and sycamores it was delightful. And peaceful. She realized how busy she had been lately. It would be a perfect morning except for one thing.

Grady turned around and saw her. If she had been uncomfortable before, it was nothing compared to now. Sparks, she thought, feeling them dance into life, igniting the air with little bits of invisible fiery tension. Sparks that made her angry, that weren't wanted or appreciated or understood. How could laughing green eyes make every nerve in her body quiver? And now she was confronted by The Chest. She wouldn't look.

He smiled, a slow lifting of the corners of his mouth that set off another shower of invisible sparks.

"Wow. What a good day this is turning out to be!"

he drawled, and she felt overwhelmed because his husky voice was as hot as the tamales simmering in the cart.

"Good morning," she said, trying with every ounce of her being to sound businesslike while she wrestled with the problem. She didn't want to look down at The Chest, but if she didn't just *glance* at it, he would tease her. Yet—the hazards Uncle Stanton had put her into!—if she looked down, casually and indifferently glancing at Grady O'Toole's marvelous chest, she knew it wouldn't be a glance. She'd be stuck like Brer Rabbit to the tar baby. She decided it was safer not to risk a glance.

His smile changed to a grin and his gaze became an appraisal that sent her temperature soaring. He looked at her breasts, her waist, her hips, her legs—all covered by the pink sundress, but she didn't feel covered. She felt as naked as he looked. And she blushed. Why in heaven did she have this reaction to him? she wondered for the umpteenth time.

"And to what do I owe the pleasure of this visit?" he asked. "Here, have a seat." He whisked the folding chair out for her and placed it in the shade of the oak.

"How's your foot?" he went on.

"It's just fine," she said politely.

"Good. My tamales are cooking, or I'd offer you one. Would you like a cool glass of lemonade?"

"No, thank you," she said, sitting down. To her consternation he plopped down on the ground, sitting cross-legged facing her. It made her feel stiff and prim to be in the chair while he was folded up on the ground below her eye level.

"Maybe we can converse better if I sit down

beside you," she said, and slipped off the chair onto the grass, folding her legs beneath her. Her pink skirt billowed out, covering his legs as well as hers. She moved it away, wishing she had stayed in the chair. This was no way to conduct business. The Chest was inches away again, unavoidably noticeable, enticing her gaze like a bright blue feathery lure in front of a trout. She was going to have to look.

Her gaze drifted down over solid muscles, smooth brown skin, short dark hair to a flat stomach, to the tight waistband of his shorts. As her gaze dropped her temperature soared.

"My, it's a warm morning," she said, fanning herself with Uncle Stanton's papers. Her gaze kept right on, down over his brown legs to the big, dusty Top Siders. She looked at Uncle Stanton's papers and smoothed them in her lap while she tried to compose herself. "My uncle is in the hospital."

"I'm sorry. I hope it's nothing serious," he said.

"It's his feet. He's had an operation on his toes, and his doctor said he needed to rest." She looked up into his eyes as she said, "I have a proposition for you."

The moment she spoke she knew she should have worded her sentence another way. His eyes developed a twinkle and his mouth curved in a lopsided grin. "Oh, Clarice! I can't wait to hear your proposition." He drew out the word *proposition*, making it sound like the most suggestive offer possible. "I'm all ears."

How could he do it to her? she wondered. Never before had she met a man who aggravated her so much, who flustered her so badly, and who made her pulse race like a car in the Indianapolis 500.

She stiffened her spine, and he looked at her breasts. She felt her body's response. Her body had no aversion to Grady O'Toole at all.

"Mr. O'Toole, this is a—"

"Grady, remember?" he said in an intimate whisper that stopped her words in mid-sentence.

"Grady. I have a business proposition for you from Uncle Stanton."

He stared at her a moment, his eyes seeming to darken and beckon her to lean closer. "What a disappointment," he said, sounding as if he meant it. "You got me all a-twitter imagining some other kind of proposition—like could we go out Saturday night."

"It's business," she said, but her voice was breathless again, slightly shaky, and she couldn't look away from his magnetic eyes. "You are," she said softly and without thought, "the most *physical* man I've ever known."

"Great day in the morning," he drawled in a husky voice that carried as much steam as the tamale stand, then leaned closer, looking surprised.

She stared at him. He frowned. He looked aggravated, she thought, but he didn't take his eyes from hers. She felt caught in an invisible net that seemed to be drawing tightly around them, pulling them nearer and nearer. His gaze lowered just a fraction to her lips, and her breathing stopped. Her gaze lowered just a fraction, and her pulse seemed to stop. What a marvelous mouth he had! She leaned forward. It was difficult to hold her eyes open, impossible to think. What would it be like to be kissed by Grady O'Toole?

On the highway yards away someone honked,

making her jump. A bright green car filled with kids passed and a boy leaned out the window to yell something unintelligible. It broke the spell that had caught her and she sat back, smoothing the papers in her lap, realizing how close she had come to doing something ridiculous.

"Now, Mr. O—Grady, what Uncle Stanton would like to do is show you three properties he owns."

Grady stared at her while she talked. "What I'd like to do, Clarice, is take you out Saturday night," he said, watching her. His voice seemed to come from far away and the words were out before he thought. He didn't want to get involved with Clarice Jenkins, he reminded himself. He blinked and stared at her, waiting while she frowned and looked down at the papers in her lap.

"Thank you, but I have to work," she said.

His mind was greatly, enormously, relieved while some little part of him he didn't want to acknowledge was disappointed. He stood up and brushed off the seat of his pants. "I have to turn the tamales."

He didn't have to. He'd just had another narrow escape. What was it with her? She was prim and proper—not his type at all. And he couldn't keep away from her! He'd been stuck with tamales too long. He'd get a date tonight if he had to post a sign under "O'Toole's Hot Tamales, Yum-Yum!" and advertise for an eligible female.

He glanced over his shoulder at Clarice and caught her looking at him. She ducked her head and her cheeks flushed. He jabbed a tamale angrily with a fork. She was as square as a cube of ice, he thought. But not as cold, a little inner voice reminded him. Nosiree, Clarice Jenkins wasn't

cold. She had wanted him to kiss her a few
moments ago, and every time he looked at her, he
could see her body's intense and immediate reaction. And it was doing things to his libido. He
wiped his brow and tried to forget how the pink top
of her sundress molded breasts that were high and
just the right fullness, thrusting more than
enough to stir him to an unbearable heat.

Think of someone else, he told himself. Peggy.
Peggy, who had been fun and beautiful, with her
long golden hair. Peggy, who had been determined
to run his life. Peggy and tamales would never have
mixed. He tried to think about Stanton Jenkins's
business proposition. And, Grady sternly admon-
ished himself in a silent debate, don't ask Clarice
Jenkins for a date. Don't kiss her. If you want to
stay out of trouble, don't flirt with her.

And the other little demon voice inside of him
snapped back gleefully, "You're going to miss some
fun, Grady. She makes your blood boil just with a
glance. How many other women can do that?"

"Plenty!" answered his Voice of Reason.

"Yeah? Name one," argued his libido. Grady
threw down the fork and turned around. She was
staring at him, her cheeks pink. He wanted to
cross the space between them and pull her up into
his arms and kiss her. He jammed his hands into
his hip pockets and rocked on his heels. "What's
the proposition?" he asked.

She tilted her head to one side. "Uncle Stanton
has three properties. Here's a list with the
addresses." She unfolded her legs in a graceful
movement and stood up, brushing off her skirt as
she came closer to hand him the list. He took it and

their fingers brushed, and he felt as if he'd thrust his hand into the pan of tamales.

He looked at the three addresses, then questioningly at her.

"If you like one of the locations," she said, "he'll sell it to you for the same price you sell this little strip of land to him, plus two thousand dollars to you."

He looked at the addresses again. Two thousand dollars, he thought. It made him angry that two thousand dollars sounded like an enormous sum, and it aggravated him that Stanton Jenkins wanted to get rid of him. But the Voice of Reason told him he could use the money, and the patch of land where he parked his tamale stand was of little importance as long as it was on a main thoroughfare. All three properties in question were. They were slightly larger, better pieces of land, and in good locations. There wasn't a reason on earth to refuse the deal. He looked into big blue eyes and saw the pink return to her cheeks.

"I like it here," he said, handing back the paper to her while his inner Voice of Reason reeled from the blow.

"That's the most unbusinesslike, bull-headed attitude! You *are* a tamale type who won't even consider a business proposition that is sound and good!"

He gripped the tamale stand and grinned at her. Why was it that the more angry she became, the more he felt like teasing her and the more he wanted to reach for her? "Think two thousand dollars!" his Voice of Reason shouted.

"All right, I'll be businesslike. I'll go look at each of the three locations before I give you an answer."

"Good."

"If you'll go with me to look at them."

She blinked and backed up a step. She was square, prim, shy, he thought, qualities he didn't care for or need in his life. Stress was doing strange things to his system.

"You can look at them just fine without me," she said.

She had the bluest eyes he had ever seen. And her lips were full, just begging to be kissed. "Nope, sorry," he said. "Tell Uncle Stanton you wouldn't go with me, therefore I refused to consider his offer."

She glared at him, keeping her eyes above his collarbones.

He scratched his chest. It didn't itch; he just wanted to see what she would do. Her lips firmed. He rubbed the palm of his hand across his chest. Her lashes fluttered. He grinned at her, knowing he was teasing her. Prim, prissy, square, old-fashioned—it was only skin deep. She was as sensual as any woman he had ever encountered.

He took a deep breath, making his chest expand, and she looked down. Her lips parted and the tip of her pink tongue came out to touch her lower lip, and he felt his arousal, a swift heat filling his loins while his pulse jumped. He turned around, working feverishly over the tamales. Clarice Jenkins was pure trouble, he thought. He ought to make the deal with Stanton Jenkins and get the hell across town from Miss Clarice-old-fashioned-Jenkins. Old-fashioned women could mess up your life, he told himself sternly, turning tamales wrapped in pale golden corn husks, bubbling in the big metal tray.

"When do you want to go?" she asked in a tone a notch deeper than her normal voice. He felt his blood bubble like tamale sauce.

"Sunday night, six o'clock," he said, knowing King's Crown was closed Sunday evening, so she wouldn't be working.

"Very well. I'll meet you here, and we'll go look at the property." Her voice had dropped even lower. And it had a raspy quality that rubbed his nerves raw. He wiped his hands and turned around to look at her.

"Give me the list again." He reached out to take it and their fingers brushed. "What's your address? I'll pick you up and we can—"

A car horn sounded and a red Porsche whipped into the lot, bouncing to a stop. A man dressed in a conservative charcoal seersucker suit stepped out and grinned. Grady felt relief wash over him like a tidal wave. "Hi, Sam," he said, watching his friend and former employee walked toward him. Blond, tall, and single, Sam took in Clarice in one sweeping glance.

"Clarice Jenkins, this is Sam Banks, a friend of mine. Sam, this is Clarice Jenkins, who works next door."

"Ah, it's nice to meet you. You're at King's Crown?"

"Yes. I'm glad to meet you. I have to run along. The lunch crowd will start coming in soon."

"I'll meet you here, six o'clock Sunday," Grady said quickly.

She nodded, looked at Sam, and said, "It was nice to meet you," turned, and left.

Grady wiped his hands on a wet cloth and busied

himself with tamales while Sam watched Clarice walk back to King's Crown.

"Who's the doll?" Sam asked.

"Thank heavens you showed up when you did. Sam, do me a favor and get me a date for Saturday night. Call one of the women you always have on hand."

"Since when don't you get your own dates?"

"I can't think of anyone. Kerri is on vacation in Alaska. Patsy moved to Cleveland. Madeline is in Dallas. Peggy and I are through."

"You sound desperate. What's the matter with what's-her-name? Jenkins?"

"Nope. Not my type."

"You're going out with her Sunday."

"Strictly business."

"I think stress has finally affected your mind. Have you taken a good look at her?"

"I know her. She's not my type." Grady worked in silence, aware that Sam had leaned against a nearby tree and was studying him.

"Why don't you junk this stupid stand and come back to the business?"

"I can't do anything until the case gets to court. What's happening?"

"How should I know?"

Grady paused to stare at his friend in shock. "You left them?"

"Bart fired me. One by one he's getting rid of everyone who was on your side when the split came."

Grady swore. "I'm sorry."

"I'll find another job."

"I know you will. You're damned good and Bart will be sorry."

"There are plenty of good men left. That's why I came by. Will you write a reference for me this weekend?"

"Sure. I'll do it tonight."

"I'm going out with Jenna Saturday. You want to come with us? She has lots of good-looking friends."

"You bet. Get me a knockout who's sophisticated."

"One sophisticated knockout coming up. I think you need to relax."

"Amen, brother."

"Did you know you've turned the same tamale exactly twelve times now?"

Shocked, Grady looked down at the tamale and dropped the spatula in disgust.

"What's eating you?" Sam asked. "Sophisticated, a knockout? I thought you were over Peggy—at least, over the worst of the breakup."

"Yeah. My mind's on business."

"Why do I get the feeling your mind's on women?"

"Yoo-hoo, Grady!"

Grady turned to see Clarice coming back at a brisk walk down King's Crown Drive. She stopped several feet from him. "I'm sorry, I forgot. I promised Kent I'd go to his softball game. Can we make it half-past six instead of six?"

"Sure. See you then."

"Kent?" Sam asked Grady.

"Her kid brother," he answered.

"You're not interested?"

"Nope!"

Sam turned swiftly, catching up with Clarice as she walked toward the kitchen door. Grady continued to get the tamales ready for noon customers. A car pulled into the cleared area and the teenage driver asked for two orders of tamales. Grady served him and completed the sale, dropping the money into a metal cash box.

Sam came back within minutes. "You sell tamales at half-past ten in the morning?" he asked.

"Kids are hungry twenty-four hours a day."

"Yeah. I'm glad I stopped. I have a date next Tuesday night with Clarice Jenkins."

"You do?" Grady shot out the question and Sam's brows rose.

"Hey, I thought you didn't care."

"I don't. I'm glad you have a date. I was just surprised because she doesn't seem your type."

"She's a good-looking woman. That's type enough. What type is she? Any perversions, I hope, I hope."

"Ha. Your hope's in vain. She is old-fashioned, prim, the apple-pie, vine-covered-cottage, trouble—real trouble—type."

"She is? You've been out with her?"

"You don't have to go out with someone to know a few things about them."

"You don't say? She didn't seem old-fashioned to me. The way she walks isn't prim. I'd say she's just the opposite. I mean, she accepted a date and she's known me only a few minutes."

"Yeah, that's true."

After a moment of silence Sam said, "I may cancel that date." When Grady looked up he added, "You're back to turning the same tamale. I don't want to come between you and Clarice."

"There is nothing between Clarice and me."

"Huh! You have enough on your mind with your cousin taking over your business and the lawsuit to get it back. You don't need one of your friends to date the new woman in your life."

Grady plunked down the spatula and put his hands on his hips.

"She's not the new woman in my life. She hates me. She calls me a tamale type. And you'd do me a favor if you'd take her out because then I wouldn't be tempted to interfere in my friend's love life. She is not my type. She's prim, old-fashioned, narrow-minded, persnickety—"

"I'm breaking our date. Wow. I haven't seen a woman get you in knots like this except for those two weeks with Peggy, and you'd gone with her a year when the breakup came."

"Don't break your date. Clarice wants to go out with you."

"She didn't really. I sort of tricked her into it. I told her King's Crown was my favorite restaurant. I love to eat there, et cetera, et cetera, and cornered her into eating with me there Tuesday night."

"Go for it. You'd be doing me a favor. I'd like to get her off my mind."

"My friend, she's quite a dish."

"She's not a 'dish.' She's all the things I've never gotten involved with in women." Grady looked at Sam, who was grinning at him. He laughed and rubbed his chin. "And I can't take my eyes off her. She does something to me when she's around."

"She might not be as old-fashioned as you think."

"She is, down to her dainty ankles. She is pure trouble, and more trouble I don't need."

"I never thought I'd see the day. Even with Peggy, it was you who wanted out of the relationship first, not her. You've got a bad case, my friend."

"Yeah. Some help you are. Keep the Tuesday date and do me a favor."

"It isn't really a bonafide date."

"She hates the tamale stand."

"Can you blame her? Do you like selling tamales? This is stupidity. You have an engineering degree, built up your own company—and here you are peddling tamales."

"Did you tell her?"

"No. Haven't you?"

"No. This is an honest business, and to tell you the truth—"

Sam groaned. "Don't say it. Don't tell me you like making hot tamales?"

"As a matter of fact, I'm doing a little better business every day I'm out here. And I feel more relaxed than I have in the past eight years. Look at this." He waved his arms and looked up at the tall oak that shaded the stand. A redbird chirped from a high branch, and a faint breeze rustled the leaves. Grady took a deep breath of air. "This is grand."

"Oh, holy birdfeathers! I think stress warped your brain. You're ga-ga over an old-fashioned woman who isn't your type, you're happy peddling tamales, you like it out here with nothing but a tamale cart and nature—holy smoke!" Sam started toward his car. "She may be right—you may have turned into a tamale type. I've got to run, because I have an appointment for an interview with Foster Drilling. I'll give you as a reference. I won't put down on the form that you're in the tamale business."

"This is honest work."

"You never could resist a challenge," Sam said.

"Wonder if Little Miss Clarice knows how you react to challenges?"

"Dammit, keep your Tuesday date!"

"You've gone around the bend. Write that reference before you forget how to write." Sam slammed the door and drove off as two customers slowed and stopped to get tamales. Grady was busy for the next three hours.

On Sunday afternoon Grady was tempted to forget about the appointment with Clarice. He paced around the living room of his condominium and argued with himself, finally deciding he would keep it, look at the property, and come home quickly. He'd call Sasha, the woman he'd met the night before when he had gone out with Sam and Jenna. Sasha was just what he needed. Tall, cool, sophisticated. He'd had a good time. He looked up her number, called her, and asked her out later that night. He replaced the receiver, feeling better. He had a date later. He couldn't get involved with Clarice. Just business and nothing more.

Thirty minutes later he drove along Apache Avenue, clutching the steering wheel of the car as if he were drowning and it were a life preserver.

Three

Grady stared at the road, inhaling perfume that smelled like a combination of roses, jasmine, and honeysuckle. It took all his effort to concentrate on driving and not look at her long tan legs. She had worn shorts, and he felt as if a bonfire had started beneath him when she had opened the door of her car and stepped out to meet him in the parking lot of King's Crown. The lady had long shapely tanned legs, enticing beyond any pair of legs he'd ever seen. He glanced at her briefly, his gaze flicking over her knees before he returned to watching traffic. Her black hair was down, tied up in a blue hair ribbon, for corn's sake! Hair ribbons, almost no makeup, fresh as a daisy, and her big blue eyes had messed up his pulse ridiculously. "She is pure trouble," said his Voice of Reason. "Look at that property in a hurry and go pick up Sasha."

He glanced at Clarice. "Are you and your uncle Stanton close? He seems to rely on you more than on the others."

"He says I have more of a head for business than Uncle Theo," she said with a smile. "Uncle Stanton and Uncle Theo are as different as flowers and shoes. Uncle Stanton is thrifty and Uncle Theo is really a little too generous for his own good. He's so sweet; he helps everyone and anyone. Dad's theory is that Uncle Stanton couldn't bear Uncle Theo's foolish generosity and overcompensated. And maybe Uncle Theo overcompensates for Uncle Stanton's thrift."

"What about your father?"

She smiled. "Dad's normal—he's thrifty at times and generous at times. He's much more solemn than Uncle Theo. Uncle Theo is like . . . sort of like Santa Claus or a big elf. There's something childlike in Uncle Theo."

"There must be something mischievous in Uncle Theo. He told the truckers to dump the dirt at the door."

Shocked, she stared at him. "I don't believe it! He isn't mischievous at all. He wouldn't do something to cause trouble. You're mistaken."

"I called and raised a little fuss with them for dumping at the door and the guy who drove the truck said, 'The curly-haired man with baby-blue eyes was standing in back at the dumpster when we started to unload at the corner of your parking lot, and he told us to pour it by the door.' "

"I can't believe it. He never causes trouble." Clarice frowned, worrying over the bit of news.

"Well, he did this time. You know he fits their description."

"He was widowed two years ago and he misses Aunt Maggie terribly. Maybe his mind was somewhere else besides on what he was saying."

After a few minutes silence, Grady asked, "Have you worked for your uncle Stanton since the restaurant opened?"

"Oh, heavens no!" She laughed, and he felt his heart do something strange. He glanced at her and warmth fanned through him. She had a gorgeous smile, and there was nothing prim in it. It was a come-hither laugh-with-me smile that made him smile in return.

"I've worked there just since he's been in the hospital," Clarice said, glancing at him. Grady was breathtakingly handsome in his casual clothes. Nothing could hide the breadth of his broad shoulders, and his open-necked blue cotton shirt and snug jeans looked great. She smoothed her fingers over her knee. She had debated whether to wear something to cover herself up or to be comfortable. Comfort had won, so she wore blue shorts and a white knit shirt.

"What did you do before?" he asked.

"I was a receptionist and secretary for a dentist, Dr. McClellan."

"Why'd you get that job?"

"I've taken courses in secretarial work. That's what I want to do because it's a solid, secure job, one that's neat and orderly."

"And how'd you go from that to King's Crown?"

"Uncle Stanton pleaded with me to come work while he's laid up. He said, 'Blood's thicker than water,' and he needed his relatives to take charge in his absence. Actually he's a little miserly and a lot suspicious of people."

"He is different from Theo."

She was surprised at Grady's remark. "You hardly know Uncle Theo."

"You just told me about him, and he's come over to talk to me every morning."

Suspicion dawned on Clarice. "He's supposed to

be trying to get you to move. Knowing Uncle Theo, I'll bet he hasn't done anything more than ask you if you want to move."

"He hasn't mentioned it at all," Grady said, and grinned.

"He hasn't?" She paused. "Well, I guess that's not really surprising."

"Do you like working at King's Crown?"

"I love it!" she said happily.

"You'll stay at the restaurant then?"

"Oh, yes! We all like working there. Kent has to go to school in the fall, but he'll work after school and on weekends."

"Do you live with your family?"

"No, I have my own apartment."

He looked surprised as he glanced at her. "You live alone?"

"Yes. Whom do you live with?" The moment she said it, she realized how the question sounded and that she might not want to know the answer, that it was a very personal question.

He laughed. "If you mean, am I married, the answer is no."

"Here's the eight-hundred block on Wilmington Boulevard, and there's the lot. See." She pointed.

"Where? All I see are buildings."

"There. Just turn—" She touched his arm and forgot what she had been about to say. The contact sent a tingle slithering through her that made her intensely aware of him. He stared straight ahead and turned the corner, circling around to come up in the alley behind the empty lot.

He parked and they both stepped out into the dusty alley. The lot was empty, but had been recently mowed, and weeds lay yellow and brittle on the ground. Two buildings flanked the lot, a music store and an upholstery shop, both closed. In the setting rays of the hot July sun they walked across the lot, weeds rustling beneath their feet while traffic whipped past on the busy boulevard.

Grady put his hands on his hips and looked at the traffic, shaking his head. "Sorry, this isn't for me."

"It's a busy location," she said, thinking how bleak it looked.

"There aren't any redbirds."

Startled, she stared at him. "What are you talking about?"

"I have cardinals in the oak trees where I am. I like that. And I like the view of the park with the swans on the lake."

"I know," she said, surprised that he would feel the same way. "It makes me feel contented when I drive in every morning and see the lake."

"Sorry. I need oaks and cardinals. What would I look at here?" His voice lowered and he came a step closer. "No redbirds, no big shady oaks, no lake, no beautiful lady with a ribbon in her hair."

He touched her cheek, his hand drifting around her neck to the ribbon. His hand slipped across the nape of her neck, and she couldn't move.

"We better look at the next lot," she said breathlessly. "It might have oaks." She hurried back to the car, feeling a sense of panic. Grady O'Toole was a disturbing element in her life, and she didn't want to become interested in a man who ran a tamale stand!

He climbed behind the wheel and they drove down the alley. "So you worked for a dentist. What did Theo do?"

"Uncle Theo drifts from job to job. He was a deliveryman at the Wooble Flower Company. Kent worked at Hamburger Heaven."

"All three of you quit jobs to work for your uncle?"

"He made us good offers and none of us were working at a place that was difficult to leave. Uncle Stanton really pleaded with us." She was becoming aware of a tantalizing smell like pines after a rain. She inhaled. It was faint, but enticing. "If we show a steady profit and an increase in business, he'll let us stay on permanently and share in the profits of the business. Except Kent isn't included, because he still has school ahead of him."

"So you'll own part of King's Crown if all goes well."

"Yes, and I like the work. I liked my job before, but this is nicer."

"What about Kent and Uncle Theo? Do they like it too?"

"Yes, we all do. Uncle Theo was a bartender years ago. He knows how to do that, and people tell him about themselves. You'd be amazed at what people tell Uncle Theo."

"Is that right?" Grady said, his cheeks growing a little pink, and suddenly she wondered what he had said to Uncle Theo.

"Usually he keeps their secrets to himself, but I know about the confidences because I've heard people talking to him. Sometimes it's been my friends, and they've told me about talking problems over with him. They tell him their deepest secrets. Uncle Theo always makes you feel better. I guess he's a good listener."

"And everyone needs a good listener now and then."

She was mildly curious about what could bother Grady enough to need a good listener. "What did you do before the tamales?"

"A little of this and a little of that," he said, and she wondered what kind of vagabond existence he'd had.

"Turn left at the next corner," she said, then she pointed at the lot. "This one has trees."

They passed it and circled the block before Grady found that there was nowhere to stop except in the busy boulevard in front. The lot was on a corner and had two elm trees on one side near the street. A park was across the street and a row of businesses next door.

"See, this place has trees!" Clarice said, staring at the lot as traffic whizzed past.

"Two trees with Dutch elm disease," Grady said, leaning close to her as he looked out her side of the car. His arm stretched along the seat behind her, resting lightly across her shoulders, his fingers on the rolled-up window. As he talked his breath fanned on her and she became more aware of him than of the lot and business. "The street is too busy for anyone to stop to buy tamales," he said, but his words had slowed and his voice had deepened. She stared at the empty lot, her heart thudding. If she turned to look at Grady, his face would be inches away, his mouth so close. . . .

"What do you think about it as a prospective site?" he asked.

She couldn't think of anything except how close he was. "It's grand," she said softly.

"Why do you think so?"

"I don't," she said, wondering vaguely if she had just contradicted herself. She tried to say something intelligent, to ignore his proximity. "This lot's not right for you. There are no redbirds, no oaks, no lake. Let's go to the next kiss—*place!*" Her face burned. Why had she said *kiss* instead of *place?*

He laughed softly. "Clarice." The word played over her nerves like a bow on fiddle strings, leaving her quivering.

"Let's go, Grady, please." She waited, but the car didn't start, and she didn't hear him move. Then his lips brushed faintly against her neck below her ear, the barest touch.

She closed her eyes in agony. "Grady, don't, please."

She heard his sigh as he moved away. After a moment he asked, "How old are you?"

She looked up at him. "Twenty-six. How—"

"I'm thirty-three, single, and happy with my tamale location." He started the car and they drove away. She felt a mixture of emotions—disappointment, excitement. "On to the next location," he said gruffly while she stared straight ahead.

After a few minutes he said, "So, you'll soon own part of King's Crown."

His voice was normal and friendly, and she relaxed a fraction. She shifted in the seat so she could watch him as she talked. "Yes, I hope so. If things keep on like they are now. We have to increase business or Uncle Stanton won't let us have a percentage. Actually we'll each get five percent to start and maybe more as time goes by."

"Five percent?" He frowned. "That's a small percentage."

"Well, there are two of us—so that means ten percent Uncle Stanton is giving up. And he pays us more than we were making at our previous jobs. We get fifty dollars more a month than we were making."

"You're working a whole lot harder, aren't you?"

"Maybe so, but I like it."

"How many more hours do you work now than you did for the dentist?"

"That was a four-day week, eight hours a day. This is six days a week."

"And how many hours?"

"A lot, but I like the work. Look at you—you work more than eight hours six days a week, and how many hours on Sunday?"

"Usually about six hours," he answered easily, and smiled at her. "But I like the work."

She laughed, wondering about him. "Where do you live?"

"I have a little place."

Because of the tamale stand she envisioned him sleeping under a bridge like a hobo, but the big black Lincoln and the clothes he was wearing indicated something more solid.

"Did you go to college?" he asked.

"Yes, and took business courses and learned how to be a secretary. I majored in personnel management, but I intended to be a secretary. I need security. Haven't you ever wanted to do something besides have a tamale stand?"

"Oh, sure. This is fairly new, but I like it."

"It's nice you like your work."

He laughed. "But you and your uncle Stanton despise it and wish I'd disappear."

She smiled coolly at him and they drove quietly

for a time. The final location was far across the city and they sped along the highway. Shortly, as they talked, she learned they liked the same type of music, and that they both enjoyed swimming and reading.

Grady signaled and turned onto the last vacant lot Uncle Stanton had to offer. It was in a newer part of the city, to the far northwest, and there was nothing around it but a large shopping mall about a mile away. The flat prairie stretched out in all directions, wildflowers blooming along the road. Grady drove across the rough ground a few yards, stopped the car, and climbed out.

She got out with him, knowing what she'd think if the offer had been made to her to move to this spot. "This will be a good location when it builds up out here," she said. "And you're near the busiest shopping mall in the city."

"Yep," he said, jamming one hand into his pocket and rubbing the back of his neck with the other. Wind caught tufts of his brown hair and tangled it above his forehead, and the scent of him, the fresh woodsy scent, became more noticeable. He looked strained, as if he were fighting some inner battle. "Do you know how long I'd have to wait out here to get a customer?"

"A year from now, this will probably be in the middle of a very good area."

"Yeah. If I were looking for an investment, it's great. Right now I'd sell two tamales a week, I imagine. Sorry, Clarice," he said abruptly, and held open the door of the car for her while he gazed into the distance.

She climbed in, feeling simultaneously disappointed and relieved that he hadn't wanted one of

ing her lips as his tongue touched, starting golden flames. Her senses reeled, and she slipped her slender arms around his neck, standing on tiptoe to kiss him back.

He surpassed all expectations. His hot kisses made her tremble and gasp with need.

Finally he released her and she stared at him in shock, realizing how deep her response had been. He looked stunned as he stared at her.

"We better go back, Grady," she said. "It's getting late."

"Yeah," he answered gruffly, taking her arm. They walked in silence to their cars.

"Thanks for the nice evening," she said.

"Sure. Let's go to dinner next Sunday night."

She glanced at his lot, the tamale stand, the folded-up banner that read "O'Toole's Hot Tamales, Yum-Yum!" She shook her head, answering wisely and a bit sadly, "There's a world of difference between us. Thank you, but I don't think we should."

"Yeah. Well, good night, Clarice." He stood beside his car while she climbed into hers and drove away.

Clarice had forgotten completely about how angry Uncle Stanton was going to be that his offer had been turned down.

Four

She didn't forget long. The phone was ringing when she entered her small apartment and she rushed to answer it. "Well, did he swap lots?" asked Uncle Stanton in his crackly voice.

"No, sir. I'm sorry," she said, thinking about Grady's green eyes.

"Dang burn, Clarice! How come you didn't sell him on the idea? He'd make two thousand dollars, besides coming out with a better lot than he has now."

"The one he has now has redbirds," she said dreamily, undisturbed by Uncle Stanton's wrath.

There was a moment of silence. "Redbirds? Birds? Little feathery critters?"

"Yes, Uncle Stanton. Grady O'Toole likes a lot with trees and birds and a view of the lake."

"Dang burn, sounds like Theo. I'll buy him a flock of birds and two trees. Offer him that, will you! Call the man right now, Clarice."

"The birds will fly away."

"Hell's bells, he could keep them in cages."

"No, sir, he likes his birds free."

"Are you all right?"

"Yes, sir," she murmured.

"You sound funny. All right, I'll get out my second line of attack. Clarice, in the morning you go right over to that hot-tamale peddler and offer him a job working for you."

Clarice was shocked. She stared at the phone, coming out of her euphoria as if she had been hit with a wave of ice water.

"You offer him an hourly wage; start low and go up, but you get him to come to work for you at King's Crown."

For a moment she said nothing. She didn't want to offer Grady a job and she didn't think he'd take it anyway. For the next half hour she discussed it with Uncle Stanton, but he remained adamant.

As she replaced the receiver, her wits were functioning again and she realized she was caught in a dilemma.

She got undressed for bed, worrying over her problems like a dog with a new bone. Common sense told her that Grady O'Toole was trouble in her life. In spite of the companionship, the similar tastes, the wild kisses . . . Her thoughts clogged, and it took another ten minutes before she got back on track. In spite of all the marvelous things about Grady O'Toole, he had a basic lifestyle she didn't like one bit. And with the volatile physical attraction between them, she knew what she ought to do for her own peace of mind. She should avoid Mr. Grady O'Toole in the future.

Relationships developed from small encounters—and safety for her lay in as few small encounters with Grady as possible.

She frowned, tapping her toothbrush on the edge of the sink. And how could she have few encounters with him if he worked for her at King's Crown? Uncle Stanton was causing trouble in her life. She tilted her head and brushed her teeth. That wasn't fair. It wasn't Uncle Stanton—it was a tamale vendor who had the ambition of a gnat who was causing heaps of trouble in her life.

The next morning, armed with intentions of making an offer that he would refuse, she marched next door. She had secured her hair in a bun on top of her head, dressed in a white blouse and simple yellow skirt, and was filled with determination to resist Grady O'Toole's charm. In the light of day her resolutions grew firmer. She frowned at the banner as it fluttered above him, announcing the yum-yum tamales.

Beneath the banner was the white tamale cart. Grady was stripped to the waist, wearing his usual brief cutoffs and big Mexican hat while he worked over his wares. And the sight of his broad-shouldered, powerful body made her resolutions go up like fog on the Sahara.

"He is a tamale type." She ground out the words softly. "Do I want to end up pining over a man who has the stability of a butterfly?" She clamped her jaw closed while her mind chanted, "Resist, resist . . ." and she became angry that she was tempted by someone so entirely different from herself.

Grady spooned tamale sauce into corn husks and rolled the tamales up. He had noticed Clarice's car when he'd arrived about thirty minutes earlier and couldn't get her off his mind, though he was trying with dogged persistence to do so. She was trouble. Pure, unadulterated trouble that he didn't need. His life was complicated enough now and Clarice-old-fashioned-Jenkins was one more problem he didn't want. "Look at last night," his Voice of Reason said. She'd befuddled him so badly, he was hours late for his date with Sasha and about as much fun as a bag of cement.

"Why did you react to Clarice?" The Voice of Reason erred in asking that question, because his libido took over immediately. He reacted to her because beneath all the old-fashioned habits was the most sensual woman he'd ever encountered. He'd stirred himself enough to kiss Sasha good night passionately, trying to get Clarice out of his system, trying to find that Clarice's kisses were nothing compared to Sasha's, only to discover that Sasha's were nothing compared to prim, old-fashioned Clarice.

If he had met Clarice a year ago, it would have been all right, but not now. She was not the casual affair type. She was as permanent as sunshine and he didn't want to get entangled with her. Blue eyes, lips that were sweeter than honey, a body that was soft and fitted to his . . . He groaned and worked faster.

"I won't!" he heard someone say softly, and turned around.

There she was. He wondered if she was a figment of his imagination. He blinked and stared at her, and she stood as still as a statue, solemnly staring back at him. Desire fanned through him with the speed of a brushfire. "Oh, damn," he said as meat dropped from the spoon he was holding onto the toes of his Top-Siders.

"Good morning," she said breathlessly, and he

fought an urge to toss aside the spoon and take Clarice into his arms.

" 'Morning," he said. "Want to sit down?" He pulled his wits together enough to unfold a chair for her.

She shook her head, coming a step closer, carefully keeping her eyes above his collarbone. She seemed to be staring at his ear, and her cheeks were pink and he wanted to laugh.

"Still scared to look at my chest?" he drawled, watching her face grow pinker.

"Of course not!" she snapped, and glanced at his chest.

He realized they had both made a mistake. Her gaze was tangible, as if she had reached out to trail her fingers across his chest. Desire fanned through him, making him ache. And he saw her reaction. The thin white blouse and lacy bra couldn't hide what was happening to Clarice. There was no way to describe what her body was doing as "prim." She sat down quickly and rubbed her ankle.

"Did you hurt your foot?"

"Mmm." She slanted a look at him. "Would you like to come to work for me at minimum hourly wage?"

The words tumbled out so fast, he knew instantly that Stanton Jenkins had sent her with the ridiculous offer. And it was on the tip of his tongue to refuse it. Then the Voice of Reason joined forces with his libido to whisper, "Take it because you'll have a chance to learn the restaurant business."

"Sure," he said aloud. "When do I start?"

Her blue eyes widened until he thought he would

be swallowed up in them. A flush changed her face to bright pink and she stared open-mouthed at him.

He realized she had wanted and expected him to turn down her offer. As a matter of fact, he thought, she had probably offered a lower starting pay than what Uncle Stanton had told her to. Too late now.

"You'll give up tamales and redbirds and oaks just like that?"

He rubbed his hand across his chest and her pink cheeks darkened. "Just like that. There are other things to look at if I work for you," he added, unable to resist teasing her while his Voice of Reason warned him to keep his mind on business.

"Uncle Stanton's an ogre to work for."

"I'll cope."

"You won't be your own boss."

"Nope," he said, and moved closer. "You'll be my boss. I'll do whatever you say."

"You'll have to wear clothes."

"Another sacrifice I'm willing to make," he said softly, watching her breathing become erratic as he squatted down in front of her. "I like your"—he paused and she looked as if she would slip out of the chair into his arms—"offer," he finished. He wondered vaguely if she had any idea how sensual she was.

"I don't think we can work together too well," she said, staring at him solemnly.

"Of course we can," he argued, rubbing his hands on his knees.

"You'll have to take orders from me."

"Wonderful."

"You'll have to wash dishes."

"Marvelous."

"Does anything ever aggravate you."

"Not much," he lied. She was aggravating him terrifically right now. He didn't want to be spell-bound by Clarice Jenkins, held immobile only inches from her, promising to wash dishes for her at minimum wage—insanity! "You'll learn the business," the Voice of Reason whispered. "You'll be with Clarice," his libido added.

"When do you want to start?" she asked.

"Today."

"My word! I don't think this is a good idea. Uncle Stanton made me offer you the job."

"I know. It's a lousy idea."

"Then why did you accept?"

"Clarice, if you don't get up out of that chair and get away from me in the next ten seconds, I'm going to have to kiss you!"

She moved with such haste, she knocked him over. He sprawled on the ground and she looked down at him in horror.

"I'm sorry. I didn't mean to knock you over."

He grinned, relieved she had broken the spell that had bound his senses and bewitched his mind. He scrambled to his feet. "I'll sell the tamales I've made and be over."

"Why don't you start tomorrow morning? That way you won't waste any tamales."

"Fine," he answered cheerfully.

"Grady." She put her hands on her hips, firmed her lips, and stared at a point on his forehead. "There's a little physical attraction between us, but we're not the same type. I'm not your type woman—you're not my type man."

"How do you know?" he asked, sending his Voice of Reason into a spasm.

"I know. You're a . . . a—"

"Tamale type."

"Well, maybe it wasn't too nice to phrase it that way, but we're not right for each other, and it's just pointless to kiss. So will you not flirt with me? Let's keep this very businesslike."

"Of course. Put your mind at rest. I won't kiss you at work."

"Good!" she said with so much relief he had to laugh. If she only knew that all her arguments just fueled what he felt for her. He still wanted to kiss her. He picked up the spoon he'd dropped and tossed it into the basket of dirty cooking utensils he took home to wash each night. He wiped his hands and turned to find her still staring at him.

"Well, I guess we have a deal," she said.

He extended his hand. "Deal it is, boss."

She studied his hand as if she had never seen a hand before. Then she shook it, and he felt the contact run right up his arm to his heart, and his Voice of Reason had to admit that maybe there would have been a safer way to learn the restaurant business.

"I'm in charge until Uncle Stanton gets back," she said. "And remember, I have a date tomorrow night for dinner with your friend."

"Have a good time," he said with a casualness he didn't feel, looking into eyes as blue as the summer sky.

"We will." She stared at him. "You have to be at work at ten."

"You get there at eight."

"I unlock and get things started and go over the books. Employees don't come that early."

"It's deserted here at eight."

"I'm not afraid."

A car pulled to a stop in front of the tamale stand and Grady dropped her hand. "I have a customer. But you've never eaten my tamales."

"Thanks, it's a little early in the morning for tamales."

"They're tasty morsels," he drawled, his mind not on tamales.

"You have a customer waiting. 'Bye."

She hurried away, and as much as he would have liked to just stand and watch her go, he had to wait on the customer.

At eight the next morning Clarice drove to work with Kent beside her. His car was in the shop for repairs to the carburetor and Uncle Theo had left early on some personal errands. Barely hearing Kent's conversation about the concert he'd just been to at the zoo amphitheater, she was in a turmoil. She had dressed in her most sedate blouse and a plain navy skirt and had lectured herself for the past hour that she would think of Grady O'Toole as just another employee. She passed the empty lot that was minus the tamale stand and the big banner and The Chest—Grady's chest. She drove into the King's Crown lot, and even though it was a gorgeous summer morning, with a bright blue sky, butterflies on the lawn, swans on the lake, and pink and purple crepe myrtles in bloom, she didn't have a shred of serenity in her being. And the cause of all her turmoil was waiting in the big black Lincoln. He climbed out as she approached, and she watched his long legs unfold. He was wearing jeans and a nice white cotton shirt, and he looked grand.

"Hey, Sis!" Kent screeched, and flung himself into the backseat.

"Clarice! Watch out!" Grady shouted, and flailed his arms.

Too late, she realized her attention had been on Grady and not on her driving, and she slammed on the brakes as she hit the big dumpster.

"Gee whiz, Clarice!" Kent said, crawling out from the back. "You should've let me drive! You ran into the dumpster!"

"Are you hurt?" she asked breathlessly, her face burning as she saw Grady clamp his jaw shut. She suspected he was trying to keep from laughing.

"Naw, I'm not hurt, but holy smoley, you had the whole lot to park in! The dumpster's as big as an elephant. Didn't you see it?"

"Of course I saw it, Kent," she snapped.

"Then why did you hit it?" he persisted, making her more angry.

"It was an accident."

Kent started laughing as he climbed out, and Grady's lips firmed more while he turned his back on her and stared at the dumpster. She wanted to shake her fist at him. He was nothing but t-r-o-u-b-l-e! He had been trouble from the first moment he had rolled his tacky tamale stand into her life.

"Hi, Mr. O'Toole," Kent said. "You're lucky you parked at the other end of the lot."

"Yeah, Kent."

"My sister, the driver," Kent said, and laughed. "Hey, Clarice—look what you did to Uncle

Stanton's dumpster. He'll blow a gasket. Wham-o—and we're parked!" He doubled over in laughter.

She stared in consternation at the dented dumpster. Her car was fine except for a slight dent in the bumper, but her car had its share of nicks and scratches and dents, and one more wasn't alarming.

"How could you not see a dumpster?" Kent asked again, and Grady turned to look at her, waiting solemnly for her answer.

"I don't know, Kent. I just didn't see it," she said, keeping her voice level.

"Wow! You need glasses! Boy, do you need glasses."

Grady bit his lip and turned his back again, and she felt her temperature jump. "Shall we get to work?"

"Want me to lead the way?" Kent asked. "I'll show you where the door is."

"Will you stop?"

"Well, if you can't see the dumpster, I don't know how you'll find the back door. I mean, there's nothing out here but space and the dumpster, and you plowed right into it—zappo!"

He cavorted and chuckled and Clarice had to hang on to her temper while Grady brushed something off his Top-Siders and kept his face averted.

"Kent, please just shut up!"

"Sure, Sis. Accidents will happen, but you better get your eyes checked."

She unlocked the door and went straight to her office, closing the door and wondering how she would get through the day. She had to go out and tell Grady what to do, and she didn't want to see him. She took a deep breath, raised her chin, and opened the door.

She could hear Grady's voice even though he was speaking softly as he said, "Kent, I don't think your sister wants to hear about hitting the dumpster. Why don't you lay off."

"Yeah!" Kent said with another fit of laughter. "I better, because when Uncle Stanton finds out, she'll be in for it."

"Your uncle will be angry?"

"Yeah, and he just won't let up on why people do something weird. He's always asking, why did you do that? What were you thinking about? Boy, Clarice's mind must have been on something besides driving."

Her cheeks felt hot and she took another deep breath as she marched into the kitchen. She had to get Kent sufficiently busy so he would forget about the dumpster.

On the way to work that morning she had told him that Grady was coming to work at King's Crown, but she hadn't broken the news to Uncle Theo. When he came into the kitchen a few minutes later and said hello to Grady, she turned around. "Grady is going to work here now."

"Welcome to King's Crown!" Uncle Theo said in his gentle voice, and held out his hand to shake with Grady. "My, isn't that nice," he added wholeheartedly, and she stared at him, wondering why he was so pleased. "Real nice."

"Thank you, sir. I see an opportunity here."

Now she had to stare at Grady, wondering what he meant. She had an uneasy feeling. The two men looked as happy as two kids in a candy shop.

Uncle Theo went into the main dining room and

she turned to help Chef Nguyen. Within minutes everyone was busy.

But not so busy that Clarice could forget Grady. He seemed to be in the same place she was no matter where she worked. He made her nervous. He made her forget what she was doing. She was aware of him every second, and she couldn't keep from watching him.

Mid-morning she was hurrying down the hall toward the kitchen when she heard Kent. "She had the whole big lot and she hit that dumpster—wham! I jumped into the back. There wasn't a car out there except Grady's."

"You don't say," Uncle Theo commented. "Only Grady's. That isn't like Clarice."

"Oh, boy! She about came unglued. She—"

Clarice stalked into the kitchen and went straight to the chef to discuss the week's groceries with him. She ignored Kent and Uncle Theo and Grady, who had turned his back the moment she appeared. All three of them became busy while she wondered how many more times she would have to hear about that dumpster.

Five

The next crisis came when it was time for Sam Banks to arrive for their dinner date. Clarice wished she never had accepted it. When he stepped through the door, she went forward to meet him.

Grady was clearing a table when he saw Sam come in. Sam was dressed in his best brown suit, and Grady remembered the day Sam had spent an enormous sum on the fine cotton shirt he was wearing.

Grady watched Clarice thread her way across the room. Her hips had the slightest sway, just enough to be provocative and make him forget the restaurant and his task. For just an instant he was tempted to go tell Sam to get lost and forget the date.

The Voice of Reason intervened in the nick of time, and he went back to work. He carried dishes to the kitchen and wondered if it had been such a good idea to come to work at King's Crown and give up his tamale stand. All he had learned today had been how to work the dishwasher, that they ran the potatoes through the dishwasher before putting them in to bake, that he could clear a table in two minutes time.

He wondered what Sam and Clarice were talking about. Sam was good-looking, as footloose as they came, and interested in attractive women. Clarice was more than attractive. Grady got a stack of clean silverware and hurried out to set a table. Clarice was sitting in the front bay window with Sam, laughing over something he had just said. Grady's Voice of Reason told him to ignore them and be thankful that Sam had entered her life. His libido might as well have been running through the dishwasher.

"Nicki," Grady said as he stopped a waitress, and gave her his best smile. "Let me wait on Clarice. She's with a friend of mine. I introduced them."

Nicki looked up into his eyes and smiled. "Sure, if you don't think Miss Jenkins will care."

"She won't mind. I promise. I'll tell her that I asked you to let me. Thanks," he added in his warmest voice, and winked at her.

Nicki smiled again and hurried past him. He picked up a pitcher of ice water, two menus and walked to the front of the restaurant.

"Hi," he said to Sam when he reached the table.

"Hey, what are you doing here?" Sam asked.

"I work here now," he said as he placed menus in front of them. "Clarice just hired me. This is my first day." Clarice frowned at him, and he wondered whether it was because he hadn't been promoted to waiter yet, or because he had interrupted them.

"Good Lord, you work here? No kidding!" Sam said, taking a menu.

"Where's Nicki?" Clarice asked.

"I talked her into letting me wait on you. I told her I'd introduced you two."

She took a menu, watched him fill her glass, then Sam's glass, with water. "Would you care for something to drink?" he asked, and Sam looked expectantly at Clarice.

"I'll have a glass of Perrier," she said.

"And I'll have a glass of red wine," Sam said. "You know what I like."

"How do you two know each other?" Clarice asked as Grady wrote down their order. He wrote slowly while he looked at Sam intently.

Sam frowned and shrugged. "We're old friends. I can't remember when we met."

Grady continued to write and Clarice stared at him. "Aren't you going to get our drinks?"

"I'm sorry. I'm new at this. Can you tell me your orders again."

"Perrier and a glass of red wine," she said evenly.

"Sure thing. The men's room is right around that corner, Sam."

"Thanks, Grady," Sam said, looking startled.

Grady left to get drinks, hoping Sam took his hint to go to the men's room. Grady didn't want Sam to tell Clarice about his life. He should have told her himself, but he hadn't and he didn't want her to hear about it from someone else. He got their drinks from the bartender and started back, slightly annoyed because Sam wasn't leaving the table and Clarice was laughing again.

"Here we are," he said cheerfully. "One Perrier— would you like me to pour it into the glass for you?"

"No, thanks," she said, and smiled.

"And one red wine for you. It should be just the

right temperature when you get back from the men's room."

Sam looked startled again and Grady stared at him intently.

"Yeah, sure. I think it's fine now."

Grady had an urge brought on by his frustrated libido to tip the glass of red wine into Sam's lap. Instead, the Voice of Reason prevailed, and Grady smiled. "Would you care to order yet?"

Without taking his gaze from Clarice, Sam answered, "We'll order later."

There was nothing left for Grady to do. He looked at Sam, who was looking at Clarice. He looked at Clarice, who was smiling at Sam.

His libido needed a tranquilizer. The Voice of Reason said, "Get out of their lives! Learn the restaurant business and forget Clarice-pure-trouble-Jenkins!"

He listened to reason and returned to clearing tables, but as he worked he couldn't resist watching Sam and Clarice. She looked as if she were having a wonderful time, and Grady was in agony.

He snatched up the order book and returned to their table. "Would you like to order now?"

"We forgot to look at the menu," Sam said, smiling at Clarice. "Of course, you know it by heart. I like fish and beef. What's best?"

She looked up at Grady. "Why don't you come back and take our orders in a little while?"

"I'll do that," he said evenly, wanting to yank Sam right out of the seat. He snatched up a tray and worked furiously, clearing a table. As he stacked dirty dishes and empty glasses, his thoughts churned. He shouldn't care what Clarice did; Sam was one of his closest friends. There were other women in the world, his Voice of Reason told him firmly. He started for the kitchen with the tray of empty dishes and glanced at her again. Sam was laughing with her over something. Grady felt on fire. He rushed into the kitchen, pushing open one of the swinging doors with a last glance at Clarice. Stepping into the kitchen, he ran into Nicki, who was carrying a tray of glasses of ice water. He reeled and lost his grip on his tray as he grabbed Nicki to keep her from falling.

"Jeez!" he heard someone exclaim before dishes and trays crashed to the kitchen floor. He looked around to see Kent standing nearby, his eyes round and a stack of clean plates in his hand. "Jeez! You ran right into her!"

"I'm sorry, Nicki!" Grady said. "Are you all right?"

"Oh sure," she said, leaning against him.

"I was looking over my shoulder, I guess."

"You can't see any better than my sister," Kent said.

A rush of Vietnamese erupted from the chef and he waved his hands. Nicki stepped away and smoothed her wet skirt. "I can't work in this."

"Go home and change," Grady said. "I'll tell Clarice and Theo."

She knelt to pick up glasses, but Grady stopped her. "You go change and I'll clean up the spill. It was my fault." He glanced up to see Kent moving around the kitchen watching him. Kent turned his back swiftly, but Grady could have sworn the kid was laughing!

"Dammit!" Grady muttered under his breath.

Kent brought him a mop and his lips were

twitching as he started to help. "You and my sister are kinda old to be acting this way. Jeez!"

"To be acting *what* way?" Grady asked in a deadly quiet voice.

Kent bent his head over spilled ice cubes and he sounded as if he might explode with pent-up laughter. "Now I know why she ran into the dumpster."

Grady worked furiously, wanting to end the conversation. "See there," his Voice of Reason reminded him. "Trouble. Give her to Sam with your blessing."

All he heard from his libido was a gurgle of agony.

"Sis has a date out there, doesn't she?"

"Yeah!" Grady finished cleaning the floor and left the kitchen, relieved to get away from Kent's comments. "Get someone else to wait on her table," his Voice of Reason said coolly.

His libido rallied on that one. "Look at her laughing with Sam! Get going, buster."

Grady hurried to their table. "Are you ready to order now before you *go—to—the—men's room*?" He drew out the words, giving Sam his fiercest glare.

Clarice disappeared behind her menu and he thought he heard her laugh. Sam's eyes grew round and he looked at Grady's shirtfront and trousers.

"Maybe *you* should find the men's room," Sam said.

Grady remembered too late that he was as wet as Nicki had been from the collision.

"I had a little spill." He glanced at Clarice, who remained behind the menu.

He leaned down to whisper to Sam, "Will you get the hell to where I can talk to you?"

"No."

Grady's libido surged forth with the strength of Atlas, and he had to fight the temptation to grab Sam by his shirtfront.

"You want," he whispered, "another reference for a—"

He stopped. Clarice had lowered the menu and was watching him. Her gaze drifted down over his wet shirtfront and trousers, and the menu went up again.

"Go!" he whispered to Sam.

The menu lowered and she looked at him curiously. He smiled and straightened up. "Would you two care to order?"

"I'm sorry," she said sweetly, but he could have sworn he heard a tinge of laughter. "I haven't decided. Come back in a little while. What happened in the kitchen? Did you fall down?"

"No. Just a small accident." He left the table, moving to a spot where he could glare at Sam, and Clarice couldn't see him.

He glared, Sam shrugged, and Clarice turned around in her chair to look at him, so he had to go back to work.

Five minutes later he saw Sam get up and head for the men's room. Another battle waged within Grady as he headed across the room to join his friend. The moment the door closed behind him, he confronted a scowling Sam. "I thought you didn't care," Sam said. "That you wanted me to keep the date."

The Voice of Reason and his libido slugged it out

momentarily and his libido won. "I didn't, but now I do."

"You had a sudden change of heart." Sam shook locks of blond hair away from his face.

"Yeah. I feel hot and cold about her."

"I'll tell you what. I need you for a reference, and we've been friends for a long time, but you make up your mind, because she's a doll."

Grady frowned. "Enjoy yourself. I don't want you to tell her about my background and the drilling business. I want to tell her myself. She thinks I'm into tamales only."

"And you want her to think that?"

"Yes, until I can tell her. I just don't want it coming from you."

"Is that all?"

"Yes."

Suddenly Sam grinned. "Set your mind at rest. We haven't mentioned you once."

Sam's happy words didn't set Grady's libido at rest. "You haven't?"

"Nope. And we won't. We have other things to talk about. No wonder you weren't taken with Sasha."

"What about Jenna?"

"Feel free to ask her out anytime you want. I plan to get to know Clarice."

"You do, huh?"

"Is this one of the moments you're changing from cold to hot about her?"

"Nope. Go right ahead. Just don't tell her my past."

"You sound as mad as hell. This is the last time I'm asking—you're sure you don't care?"

The question hung in the air. "No, I'm not sure," Grady finally said.

"I knew it! Damn, what rotten luck."

"Look at this! She's making my life miserable, but I can't stand to watch her in there having fun with you. Maybe if you just didn't date her right under my nose, I could take it."

Sam threw up his hands and left, pushing open the swinging door that led out. He came right back in through the other door, his hands on his hips as he glared at Grady. "Why don't you date her if she's got you in knots?"

"I don't want to date her," Grady said, and his Voice of Reason began to recover. "She's prim, she's old-fashioned, she's trouble."

Sam tilted his head at an angle and the silence deepened between them. "Let me know when to come to the wedding," he bit out, and pushed through the door.

Wedding. Grady's Voice of Reason screamed in pain. Grady pried open the In door and stepped in front of Sam.

"You date her. Just go where I won't see you."

A man passed them, going into the men's room and looking at them with curiosity. Kent was standing nearby with a tray of dirty dishes, staring round-eyed at Grady.

"Uh-huh," Sam said. "Sure, I'll date her. And I'll run over you with my car tomorrow."

"I mean it," Grady said grimly, clinging to the Voice of Reason.

"Damn, I wish you had told me this before I got to know her better."

"I'm telling you, date her."

"Shh, people are staring. She's staring."

"Look what she's doing to me. I'm up to my elbows in dirty dishes. I've knocked someone down and spilled a tray of drinks. I'm wet all down my front. I'm making minimum wage while I suffer. I mean suffer. She is pure trouble. You take her off my hands and when the fever abates, I'll thank you." His Voice of Reason cheered.

"Okay, but remember, you told me to go ahead and ask her out."

"Right."

"To save you from trouble."

"Right. All I ask is that you don't tell her about my past."

"It's a deal," Sam said solemnly, extending his hand. They shook hands as the man came out of the men's room and passed them, looking even more curiously at them. They glanced at the table in the bay window.

"Dammit, she's gone!" Sam said.

"Probably went to powder her nose."

"I don't know. We've been talking a long time."

They parted and Grady returned to the kitchen to find Clarice talking to the chef. He busied himself with cutlery until she walked to the cabinet to get down some clean glasses. "You have a date. Are you going to serve yourself?" Grady asked her.

"I gave up on him. I got tired of waiting," she said coolly.

His first feeling was elation; then reason intervened and he frowned at her. "It was my fault," he said. "I talked to Sam a long time."

She turned to face him and her blue eyes were snapping with fire. "If you are trying to get him to date me, I would appreciate it if you wouldn't meddle in my life. I can get my own dates, thank you!"

"You think—? Oh, no!"

"And what else would you spend so much time discussing with Sam in the men's room? What else wouldn't keep until later? I know you were threatening him."

"I wasn't threatening him."

"Just answer me honestly. Did you tell him to date me?"

"Well, hell's bells—"

"Did you? Yes or no!"

"Yes, but it's not like you think."

She flounced away and he shrugged. She was trouble in every pretty little inch. He returned to the dining area, where Sam was waiting at their table.

"I told you she was trouble," Grady said. "She's in a rage because she thinks I'm forcing you to ask her for a date."

"She *what*? Why would she think something dumb like that?"

"How would I know how a woman's mind works? Do you want to order?"

"Hell, no! Where is she?"

"I don't really know."

"You've ruined one of the best dates I've had in a long time."

"I'm sorry. If you'd gone to the men's room when I first suggested—"

"For the sake of past friendship, I'm giving you a minute's warning," Sam said tensely. "Get out of my sight."

Grady went. He knew Sam well and he didn't want a fight to erupt because of Miss Trouble.

"See there, see there," his Voice of Reason

cackled. "She's trouble. Even on a date with another man, she's trouble!"

His libido whispered, "Go find her."

He found her trying to push a sack of trash into the dumpster.

"You shouldn't do that," he said, taking the bag of trash and slinging it into the dumpster. "Let me or Kent handle the trash."

"I really wanted a breath of fresh air and to be alone if you don't mind!"

She was glaring at him, spots of pink in her cheeks, her blue eyes flashing, and he still wanted to reach for her. He grinned and shrugged. "I'm sorry."

"If you're truly sorry, get out of my life."

"I didn't know I was in it. Does this mean you're firing me?"

"No!" she said angrily, and he knew she would like to. Uncle Stanton was the only thing that saved him.

"Okay, boss," he said, smiling at her. His Voice of Reason told him to get inside while he was ahead. His libido urged him to see how deep her anger ran.

He leaned a little closer, looking at her more intently as he smiled.

Something flickered in her blue eyes. He gazed at her lips and raised his brows quizzically. Her soft pink lips parted and he felt a flame start.

"How angry are you?" he drawled in his deepest voice.

She licked her lips and blinked, lashes momentarily hiding her wide blue eyes.

"Angry enough," she said, but the fire was no

longer in her eyes, and the snap was gone from her words.

"Angry enough for what?" he asked, wishing now they were on the back side of the dumpster and out of sight from the restaurant.

"Nyaa, nyaa, Clarice loves Grady!" came a twangy voice from the back door of the restaurant. Kent jumped inside, slamming the door behind him.

"Oh!" She quivered with rage and the fire was back in her eyes, and he had to fight laughter.

"Don't blame me for him!" he said, knowing if he grinned, he'd be sunk deeper than the *Titanic*.

"Men!" she roared, and brushed past him with her chin in the air, hurrying to the restaurant. He leaned one elbow against the dumpster, his hand on the side of his head as he enjoyed watching her storm back inside, her skirt flouncing with each step, her hips swaying provocatively.

At the door she glanced over her shoulder and caught him watching her. He smiled and waved, and she slammed the door with such force, the kitchen window rattled.

He laughed softly. "Grady, you're nuts," he said to himself. "She's still trouble."

He went back to the restaurant and she was nowhere in sight. He cleaned in the kitchen until Kent came in.

"Hey, Kent. You better leave your sister alone."

Kent grinned. "Sure, I will."

In a few minutes Grady went into the dining area to clear tables, and he stopped in shock.

Six

Clarice and Sam were together at the table by the bay window again. Grady frowned and started toward them, when a blond waitress stopped him. "I'm supposed to wait on Miss Jenkins and her friend," Tiffany said. "She told me she wanted me, no one else, and to tell you."

"Is that so?"

"Look, it was her idea, not mine."

"Oh," he said, startled that he had sounded gruff to Tiffany. "Sorry. That's fine with me. Go right ahead."

"Sure," she said, studying him with questioning eyes.

He cleared a table, looking at them surreptitiously. Clarice had chosen well. The tables in front by the two bay windows were isolated. It was an elevated area, almost an alcove, with an identical one like it on the other side of the entryway. And the nearest tables all had customers and none needed clearing away. Grady felt as if someone had lighted a slow fuse beneath him. He worked furiously, trying to forget her, wondering how Sam had gotten back in her good graces.

Later, when he saw them get up, all he felt was enormous relief. Sam disappeared through the arched doorway to the front entrance, and Clarice threaded her way back toward the hall and the cubicle she called an office. She reappeared in a few minutes, her purse strap over her shoulder, her hand resting on the white purse at her side as she walked purposefully to the front of the restaurant. It dawned on him that she was leaving with Sam.

Grady hurried across the room to step in front of her.

"I'm leaving," she said, and lowered her voice to a whisper. "Don't make a scene. I have never known anyone who could so easily cause so much trouble wherever he goes!"

"Me? Trouble?" Grady asked in shock. "You're calling *me* trouble?"

"Look. You've worked here one day and I've hit the dumpster, you knocked Nicki down as well as two trays of dishes, you caused a scene, you almost ruined my date . . . Can you just turn around and walk to the kitchen and let me get out of here without another disaster?"

"I didn't try to get him to date you. I just agreed it was okay if he did."

"That's wonderful. I understand. You're my employee. Will you take the tray you're holding and go to the kitchen?"

"Sure, in just a minute. Go out with me Friday night."

"You'll be working Friday night and Saturday night. Please, go to the kitchen now."

"Go out with me Sunday."

"People are staring," she whispered, "and you're

causing a scene. What is it about you that trouble just follows wherever you go?"

"Said by a woman who is the embodiment of trouble! I lead a simple life."

"Oh, sure you do. Since that tacky tamale stand wheeled into my life, I've gone from one dilemma to the next! Dirt in the hall and you in my hair!"

Her voice had risen on the last words, and nearby someone laughed. Grady made a sweeping bow, ushering her past him. As she walked away, he said, "I'll wheel my tamale mentality out of your life as of now. I quit!"

She whirled around, and her purse swung out and hit a customer on the side of the head. The man yelped, jumped, and knocked over his water. Grady was convulsed with laughter that he knew he better not release.

Clarice turned beet-red. "I'm so sorry," she said to the man. "I didn't mean—my purse—I'm terribly sorry. Dinner's on the house. I'll have someone show you to another table. Are you hurt?"

"No, no. I'll be fine," he said, rubbing his ear.

"We can eat right here," the woman at the table said.

While they talked, Grady picked up the fallen glass and the man's plate that was filled with water. Tiffany appeared and quickly set a nearby table for two.

"We have a place set for you at that table," Clarice said. "The tablecloth will be dry."

"Clarice?" Sam asked as he joined them. "What happened?" He glared at Grady.

"Just a minute, Sam, and I'll be with you," she said. "I have to see about these people."

As she turned to talk to them at their new table,

Sam looked at Grady. "You did something to keep her from going out with me."

"No, I didn't. She hit that guy with her purse."

Sam's eyes widened. "I don't believe you. She must have been trying to hit you."

"No, she wasn't."

At that moment Clarice returned. Grady gathered up the wet tablecloth and the glasses.

"See what I mean about your being *trouble*?" she retorted.

"I didn't do a thing except tell you good-bye," Grady said.

"Grady said you hit a guy with your purse," Sam added.

She closed her eyes and rubbed her brow. "I'll tell you about it in a minute. Shall we go?"

"Sure! 'Bye, Grady. Happy dishwashing."

The last remark grated on Grady's nerves, and he watched the two of them leave. At the arched doorway Sam dropped his arm across Clarice's shoulders and Grady wanted to hurry after them and push Sam away.

He worked diligently until closing time and drove home, glumly aware that he was tied in more knots than he cared to acknowledge.

The next morning Clarice dressed in a black skirt and a white blouse with a sailor collar. She tied her hair at the nape of her neck with a black ribbon and tried to avoid thinking about the day ahead. The phone rang and she picked it up to hear Uncle Stanton.

"Clarice? You didn't come by my room with the receipts last night."

"I thought Uncle Theo and Kent were bringing them."

"They did. And they told me some strange tales. They said you knocked a customer in the head with your purse."

She smiled. She would not let Grady and his penchant for trouble upset her.

"I turned around and my purse flew out and hit him. It didn't hurt him and we made amends—"

"You *gave* away a dinner."

Closing her eyes, she wished she could forget yesterday. "Take it out of my pay," she said, trying to keep her smile.

"I intend to. Don't give away dinners."

"Suppose he had sued us?"

"Can't sue over a flip of a purse. How'd he know you weren't a customer?"

She blinked, realizing the man wouldn't have known. "He didn't."

"That's right! No need to give away two free steak dinners. Theo told me it was steak."

"Sorry, but I'll pay for the dinners."

"Yep. What were you doing out there with your purse anyway?"

"I was talking to Grady O'Toole. I told you, Uncle Stanton, the man is a walking disaster. Things just happen when he's around. Can I fire him?" She held her breath. If Uncle Stanton let her fire Grady, then she wouldn't have to tell him Grady had quit.

"Great day in the morning, no! Yesterday was the first time in over two weeks we haven't had that dinky little tamale stand in front of my elegant restaurant. Don't you fire him and don't you let him quit!"

"Yes, sir," she said, wondering if the additional pay was worth it. The dentist's office had been calm. There had been no Grady O'Toole near the dentist's office.

She drove to work, feeling a knot of tension forming as she approached the drive. Shock hit and she stared. A horn blared and she realized she had almost drifted over into another lane. She signaled and turned into the drive as her temperature soared.

Slamming on her brakes, she climbed out, somehow remembering to smile. There was The Chest! He was back at his tamale stand.

"What are you doing?" she asked, trying to avoid looking at his body.

"Enjoying redbirds and oaks. I guess I belong in the great outdoors."

In a quandary, she bit her lip. Uncle Stanton wanted Grady in no uncertain terms. She didn't. Resisting the pull, because she wasn't going to look at The Chest, she said, "Please come back to work."

He knelt down to twiddle with something on the wheel of the tamale stand.

"Sorry."

"I'll give you a raise."

He looked over his shoulder at her. "Go out with me Sunday night."

"You're not serious!"

"Yes, unfortunately, I am."

"Since when does a man with a bod—" She felt on fire. What was the matter with her? And out came his slow grin and the twinkle in his eyes.

"With my what?"

"Have to blackmail someone into going out on a date?"

"With my what?"

"You know what!" she blurted out, wiping her brow.

He laid down the spatula and the towel he'd been holding in his hand. Each movement was deliberate, and she felt as if she couldn't get her breath. He came closer and she backed up a step into the trunk of the oak tree. He rested one hand on the trunk over her head.

"Grady . . ." The word was a rasp.

"Clarice, something happens when we're around each other and I just can't resist. You need to laugh more, you know it?"

"Laugh?" Her mind had stopped functioning. The Chest was inches away, Grady's green eyes were fathomless, and his lips were so enticing.

"Yes. That night when we ate, after looking at the lots, you finally relaxed and laughed, and it was enough to warm the North Pole. But I never see you laugh at work or during the day."

"Of course I do!" She laughed, and it sounded feeble and ridiculous.

"Not that kind of laugh. That's forced. The real kind."

"And you're going to rush into my life and make me laugh and be human!" She felt as if she were clinging to the last shred of her wits. Her gaze lowered and she was trapped. She stared at his marvelous chest that was all muscle and coppery flesh, and she wanted to touch him.

He tilted her chin up, and when she looked into his eyes she knew he was going to kiss her. And she wanted him to more than she could remember wanting anything in a long, long time.

"Go out with me Sunday night," he said.

"If you'll come back to work at King's Crown," she said.

He smiled and touched her cheek with his finger. "Now, why would someone resort to blackmail who has a bod—"

"Grady!"

"Clarice, you're tied up in knots."

"No one has accused me of that before."

"Not ever?"

"No. I don't have this problem with other men. Are you . . . coming to work?" she asked breathlessly.

"Sure," he answered.

With each statement he had come a little closer, and now there was no space left between them. She closed her eyes as his lips touched hers. So light, just a faint pressure, but she felt a reaction down to her toes.

"Mmm," she murmured, and slipped her hands over his shoulders.

A car horn blared, she heard a squeal of tires, and she looked around as Grady stepped away. To her horror she saw Kent in his old green car trying to turn into the drive—the drive that was blocked by her car.

Kent had slammed on his brakes and he skidded, the driver behind him blaring his horn and trying to brake.

"Oh, no!" she gasped, watching the green car plow into the back of her red one as the car behind Kent swerved and kept going. The driver made obscene gestures at them, which Kent immediately returned.

Kent climbed out, shaking his blond hair away from his face as he threw up his hands. "My car!"

She hurried to her own car, going around to the back. "Kent, I'm sorry. I just stopped for a minute."

"Sis, can't you get the car out of the way before you make out?"

"Kent!"

"Well, what would you call it? I saw you kissing him. Look at my fender and my bumper!"

Grady came up and viewed the disaster. "Let's see if we can get the cars apart."

"If I back up, it'll pull the bumper off my car, the way they're tangled. Mine's on top."

At that moment Uncle Theo came along, driving at his usual slow speed, a string of cars behind him as he slowed and waited, unable to turn into the drive.

Clarice wanted to vanish or to wave and shout, It's Grady O'Toole's fault!

"You stand on her car's bumper to push it down," Grady said, "and I'll lift the front end of your car up. Clarice can back your car away from hers."

"Ha! I'm not standing on any bumper with my sister behind the wheel."

"Kent, for heaven's sake! I won't hit you. I'll back your car up and we can get the bumpers apart."

"Aw, boy. Remember the dumpster."

"Get up there," she said, and went to the driver's side of his car. Kent stood on her bumper and Grady lifted, muscles straining in his arms and back. "Slowly," he called, and motioned to her. In seconds the cars were apart and Clarice got out of

Kent's car. "I still need to talk to you," she said to Grady.

"Park on my lot out of his way."

She did. Grady watched her, his gaze drifting over her legs as she stepped out of the car. She tried to sound brisk and businesslike as she asked, "Now, will you please come back to work?"

"Yep," he said casually. "And we have a date Sunday, right?"

She had to laugh. "Yes!"

He came closer. "See, that's what I mean. You need to laugh like that."

"Sure. I'm not all that solemn."

"Yes, you are."

"I come from a solemn family. My dad's as solemn as Uncle Stanton."

"Theo's not," Grady said, moving a little closer.

"No. They grew up in a tough situation, where all three of them had to start work early in life," she said, aware that Grady was smoothing her collar, tracing his finger along her throat to her ear. "My grandparents had poor health and little money to raise three boys." Her words were slow as her attention was divided between what she was trying to explain and what Grady was doing with his slight touches. "I think that's partly what's made Dad and Uncle Stanton so solemn. And probably why Uncle Stanton is a little miserly."

Momentarily she thought about her job and said, "At work I've been trying hard to do everything right. I want to keep this job because I like it better than my secretarial work, and I want to prove that I can do a good job. Uncle Stanton said he was counting on me."

"You're doing a good job, so relax," Grady said, and squeezed her shoulder lightly.

"That's easy for a tamale vendor to say!"

He shrugged. "If you're doing your best and things are running smoothly, there's no need to be uptight. I guess I'll come to work tomorrow."

"Why not today? We need you."

He grinned. "You mean Uncle Stanton doesn't want my tamale busines operating today. I have tamales cooking and I'll have to go home and get some clothes, unless you want me to come to work like this."

"Oh, no! You have to dress."

"What about my tamales?"

"Can't you take them home and freeze them?" The moment she asked, she realized he might not own a freezer.

"I can freeze them for you at the restaurant," she added hastily. "And Uncle Stanton said you can have a raise." She knew Uncle Stanton would have an attack if he found out she was offering a raise unnecessarily.

Grady grinned. "That's great."

"How's fifty cents more an hour?"

"Grand," he said with enough amusement in his expression that she began to feel uncomfortable.

"What did you do before the tamale business?" she asked.

Grady stared at her a moment. Here was a perfect chance to tell her about his background, but some perverse instinct wanted Miss Clarice-trouble-Jenkins to like him as a tamale vendor—not as an engineer and past president of his own company.

"A little of this and a little of that," he said.

"That's kind of vague," she said, wrinkling her nose in disdain.

"And you don't approve of any work that isn't as solid as concrete."

"Well, as a matter of fact, that's right. I want security."

"I'm sure you do," he said. His Voice of Reason said, "See there, see there."

"And you don't approve of my attitude," she said matter-of-factly.

He shrugged. "You have to take a risk every now and then. You took one when you left your dentist."

"Oh, no, I didn't. His wife's filling in and he's keeping the job open for me until Uncle Stanton gets out of the hospital. And this is more money than the secretarial job. I didn't take a risk at all. I want to know where I'm headed and how I'll get there."

"You didn't know where you were headed when you hit the dumpster," he drawled, moving closer again.

"You know what I mean!" She turned around to go to her car, and would have bumped into a tree trunk if Grady hadn't caught her and pulled her to one side.

"Careful," he said, still holding on to her arm." "You didn't know where you were headed then."

"And consequently, I almost hit the tree. It's wise to be cautious."

"Cautious, responsible, careful, old-fashioned, solemn—we have some similarities and some differences."

"Differences as big as the Atlantic Ocean and the Sahara Desert."

He leaned closer and his voice deepened. "Similarities like an attraction between us that makes us both forget reason and logic; that makes my pulse skip as fast as yours; that makes me want to kiss you as badly as you want to be kissed." He crossed the final tiny space to put his mouth on hers and show her some more similarities that were absolutely marvelous.

Finally she remembered where she was and what she was doing. "Grady! Stop kissing me."

He stared at her momentarily before he released her.

She smiled, wanting to fling herself back into his arms. Instead, she tried to keep her voice light as she said, "See you inside."

"Sure," he said.

She slammed her car door and hummed a tune as she drove slowly down the drive and around the curve leading to the parking lot. Her singing stopped abruptly when she saw fluttering signs, crudely lettered and tacked to the building, lampposts, and trees on the edge of the lot.

CAUTION—DUMPSTER AHEAD!

"Kent . . ." she muttered, then saw in the rearview mirror Grady pulling the tamale stand to the back of the lot.

DANGER—LARGE OBSTRUCTION! read the next sign, and she suddenly laughed at the warnings.

She parked and climbed out as Grady came across the lot with potholders in his hands, carrying a tray of steaming tamales.

He grinned. "I see Kent is interested in protecting the dumpster."

"My brother needs to grow up," she said with a smile, and Grady raised his eyebrows.

"Did I hear a laugh? I figured you'd be annoyed," he said lightly, but he was studying her intently.

"It's too pretty a day to be annoyed," she said, feeling happy with the world, aware of Grady, remembering his kisses down to the most breathtaking tiny detail.

"Well, son-of-a-gun!"

She opened the door and he went inside, putting the tamales on the counter to cool.

"Hey, Sis—neat driving."

"Kent, go out and take down the silly signs."

"What's lover boy doing here?"

"Do you want a job here?" she asked, hoping to give enough of a threat to put an end to Kent's teasing.

"Yeah."

"Then please cool it with your remarks about the dumpster."

"Yeah, sure. You don't have much sense of humor."

She looked up to see Grady standing in the doorway, one arm resting on the jamb as he listened to the conversation. Watching Kent go outside to remove the signs, she asked, "Suppose I were like him?"

"Perish the thought!" Grady answered with a grin, and left to get the next tray of tamales.

Clarice looked at the tray of steaming tamales, golden husks showing beneath a red sauce. Hunger suddenly struck; the tamales smelled too tempting to resist. She got a plate and helped herself to one, carefully unwrapping it and wiping her fingers before she cut into it to take a bite.

It was marvelous. She closed her eyes, relishing the bite.

"That good, huh?" Grady drawled in a deep voice, and her eyes flew open to find him watching her.

"Oh, yum-yum!" she drawled back, then realized she had said just what was on that tacky banner of his.

He smiled and set down another pan. Curls of steam rose from the bubbling tamales.

"That's all of them," he said. "Eat all you want."

"I just wanted a taste. Maybe we should make you assistant chef."

"Sorry, I have a limited repertoire. Tamales, chili, nachos, tossed salad, steak, barbecued chicken. That's about it."

"You like Mexican food?"

"Yep. I have a good recipe for tamales and I found a stand at a moment when I needed work."

"Want to give us the recipe? We could add tamales to the menu?"

"Sorry. I may want to go back into business. The recipe's my secret. I'll go home now and change clothes. Want to go with me?"

Suddenly she felt torn by indecision. The answer that rose to her lips was no, but she felt a deep-running curiosity about him and could picture him sleeping only under a bridge at night.

When she didn't answer immediately she received another shock. He was surprised. He hadn't expected her to accept his offer, but was merely teasing her. He *must* live under a bridge or in a hovel, she thought, and of course he wouldn't want her to see. He might live in his Lincoln and have all his belongings in the backseat and trunk!

"No, I better stay here," she said politely, and he

looked enormously relieved. He let out a long breath and smiled.

"I'll be back soon," he said, and winked at her. The wink warmed her more than the tamale. She watched him cross the lot to his car. She imagined him driving out of sight, stopping at a gas station and changing in the men's room, then returning to work. He looked as footloose and fancy-free as a cloud.

"Dreaming of Grady again," a voice said behind her, and she heard kissing sounds as Kent passed the open doorway.

"Kent!" She hurried to the hall, but he was out of sight.

Chef Cuong Nguyen came in the back door, greeting her with his usual polite smile, and they went to work. Although she was busy when Grady returned, she knew the instant he entered the kitchen. The whole day was pleasant, and would have been perfect if Sam hadn't appeared.

He came at five-thirty and the first Grady knew about his presence was when he looked up to see Sam talking to Clarice at the front of the restaurant.

She had to seat four customers and Sam leaned against the wall, watching her and waiting for her return. He didn't see Grady coming until he was beside him.

"I've changed my mind," Grady said.

Sam turned around. "Hi. Are you quitting and going back to tamales? Or back to drilling—"

"Shh! Will you stop talking about the company?"

"Oh, still haven't told her, huh?" Sam asked, but he didn't seem interested in an answer and returned to watching Clarice.

"I've changed my mind about Clarice. I don't want you to take her out."

Sam's head turned, and he focused on Grady as if he hadn't seen him in years. "Well, friend—" And then in a low voice he made a suggestion that Grady ignored.

"I talked you into taking her out," Grady said in a determined tone. "I introduced you to her and now I've changed my mind."

"It's too late."

"Look, Sam—"

"You look. I'm making headway with the most exciting woman—"

"What do you mean, making headway?" Grady snapped, his hands on his hips as he glared at Sam.

"Don't use that tone of voice with me. It's none of your business what I mean. You don't have the slightest little claim on Clarice."

"Look—"

"Here she comes. You better go back to work because it aggravates her when you stir up trouble. You know, I never knew you were a troublemaker."

"I didn't know you were one either."

"And if you're going to threaten to refuse me a reference, I have a job."

"I wouldn't do that even if we do have our differences. You're a good worker."

"Thanks, now you better go." Grady went, but to only a few yards away, where he could clear a table and watch Clarice and Sam. His thoughts were seething, his libido was in agony, and the Voice of Reason had deserted him.

He carried a tray of dirty dishes to the kitchen, taking one last look at Clarice and Sam before the door swung shut behind him. Sam's words rang in his mind, dealing blows to his libido.

". . . making headway . . ." *Headway?* Grady tossed down the potholders as the chef washed his hands and hung up his apron. Cuong was through for the night and smiled at Grady as he turned to go.

"Good evening. Will you turn the fire off under skillet? I go now."

"Sure, 'night, Cuong." Grady drummed his fingers on the counter and clamped his jaw shut. It was three days until his date with Clarice. Three days was a long time.

Seven

The next morning Clarice took a deep breath as she sat near Uncle Stanton's bed. He was propped up against white pillows, his straight brown hair combed and smoothed flat, parted in the middle. The white sheet was pulled to his waist. He wore his maroon pajamas and had his glasses on, and was gazing at the papers in his hands. In a straight chair a few feet from the hospital bed, Uncle Theo sat quietly beside her, his hands folded in his lap, his blue shirt and blue cotton slacks intensifying the blue of his eyes.

She had asked about Uncle Stanton's health and listened to a long diatribe on his toes, then she had given him the receipts of the day before and watched him settle into a slightly better frame of mind. Smoothing her yellow skirt, she said a small prayer of thanks that business had been steadily increasing at King's Crown. She was going to need everything on her side when she broke the news of what had happened last night while she had been standing out front talking to Sam.

"Uncle Stanton, I want to fire Grady O'Toole," she said.

"Nonsense! Finally got the tacky tamale stand away from King's Crown! You keep him on the payroll."

"He can't stay. He causes too much trouble."

"Trouble? Ha," he said flatly, as close as she had ever seen him come to laughing. "If you can't lick 'em, join 'em. Or get 'em to join you!" He thrust out his jaw. "Grady O'Toole stays."

Clarice glanced at Uncle Theo, who stared out the window at the sunny, well-kept hospital lawn. She took another deep breath. "Grady has to go. He set fire to the kitchen last night."

"He *what*?" Uncle Stanton sat straight up, his face turning a deep red.

"It was accidental. He tossed down some potholders where Cuong Nguyen had the fire turned low and they caught on fire and—"

"How bad is the damage?" Uncle Stanton asked angrily.

"It's minimal. It smoked up a corner of the kitchen. He had it out before the fire department came."

Uncle Stanton fell back on the pillows. "Take it out of his pay. Do you think he did it deliberately?"

"Oh, no!" she said quickly.

"He said his mind was on other matters," Uncle Theo chimed in, trying to be helpful. "Kent said the man's in love."

Clarice felt a blush start at her throat and fan up through her cheeks.

"Rotten luck," Uncle Stanton muttered, twisting the sheet in his fingers. "Just rotten luck he owns the lot next door. We have to keep him employed."

"It'll mean trouble," Clarice said. "Absolute trouble."

Uncle Stanton leaned over the side of the bed. "Then you just stay near him, missy! You be there when he comes to work and you stay until he goes, and you watch what he's doing, y'hear!"

Clarice wondered if fate was determined to wreck her life. "Yes, sir."

"Get a camera and take a picture of the kitchen and let me see it. When will it be fixed up?"

"Today. I made arrangements to get the smoke cleaned out and we have to get a new window shade—"

"Actually we were quite lucky," Uncle Theo said. "Only a few people were in the dining room and the fire was out—"

"Lucky? Rotten luck! I'll do something to get that property. But until I do, you keep Grady O'Toole at your side, Clarice!"

"Yes, sir," she answered with mixed emotions.

An hour later Clarice ushered Grady O'Toole into her office and closed the door. There was a table with a typewriter and two folding chairs in the center of a room filled with boxes and stacks of papers and miscellaneous items, including a rusty coffee urn and two boxes of chipped china cups.

"Have a seat. I need to talk to you."

She tried to sound as businesslike as possible as she went behind the table and sat down, moving the neat stack of correspondence she had typed recently.

He sat down, placing one ankle on his other knee, a hand resting on his jean-covered thigh. He wore Top-Siders, jeans, and a cotton shirt, and looked casual, appealing, and cool. And in just two seconds he made her feel ridiculous in asking him to her office.

He bothered her with his direct stare, making her wish she had let the whole matter drop.

"I need to talk to you," she began.

"Clarice!" Uncle Theo called from the front of the restaurant.

"Just a minute, please," she said, aware that Grady watched her as she stood up and crossed the room to the door to open it. She addressed Kent, who was sweeping in the hall. "Will you tell Uncle Theo I'm busy right now."

"Sure."

She closed the door and had started back to her makeshift desk when she heard Kent yell, "She's shut in with Grady. They're busy doing *something*." On the word *something* his voice rose and he drew it out until she wanted to shout at him to shut up. Instead, she tried to cling to dignity and face Grady O'Toole.

Grady bit back a laugh when he heard Kent's answer, enjoying the pink in Clarice's cheeks.

"I'll have to take the expenses for the kitchen out of your pay," she said.

"I'll cover the damages to the kitchen. I told you that last night." He ached to do something to make her smile, remembering the night they had looked at lots. She had been fun, exciting. . . . His blood began to heat, and he frowned when he thought about Sam taking her out.

"I've talked to Uncle Stanton." She rolled a pencil in her fingers and stared at it, looking uncomfortable. Finally she looked at him. "Will you keep your mind on work?"

"Sure," he said, and smiled. "Don't I always?"

"You didn't when you set the kitchen on fire."

"When's your next date with Sam?"

"Next—what difference does that make?" She picked up a piece of paper. "Will you please fill out this employment application?"

"Why? I already have the job."

"We might need your phone number."

He grinned and took the application, folding it neatly to put it into his pocket. "I'll get it back to you."

"I'm sorry you have to pay for the kitchen. That's Uncle Stanton's demand."

"How come your uncle keeps you padlocked out of his office and you have to use this closet?"

"I really don't know."

"Something secret in there?"

"Oh, heavens, no! I'm sure Uncle Stanton just wants to keep everyone out of his things. He's a little cranky."

"He should take up the tamale business. You learn how to relax."

She smiled at him, tapping her fingers on the desk. He knew she wanted him to go, but he was enjoying himself. For once he had her all to himself, and he intended to make the most of the moment.

"You can go back to work now," she said politely.

"You're not going too?"

"I have a letter to type."

"I thought Uncle Theo wanted to see you."

"Oh! Well, I guess he does. I forgot about him." She blushed and stared at Grady, and he bit back a smile.

She lifted her chin and stood up, moving with determination. He also stood, and stepped quickly into her path. She stopped instantly, just as he hoped she would, and he braced one arm on the wall, hemming her in between table and wall and himself.

"I saw the schedule," he said. "I don't work tomorrow night. Go out with me then."

"Grady, I think—"

"Clarice," he drawled, leaning closer, inhaling a faint scent of jasmine and roses. "We had a good time before . . . the best time I've had in a long, long time," he said softly.

"Grady, I—" she began, but all the force had gone out of her voice.

"You're fighting yourself. Part of you wants to go. I can see it in your big blue eyes."

"When we're together disasters happen." Her words were slurred, drawn out, and a tone deeper than usual. Her head was tilted back and she looked at him in a manner that made the room seem like a tiny furnace.

Clarice could barely get her breath. Remember, he's trouble, she reminded herself, but all she could see were his sea-green eyes, his lips, so kissable, and the marvelous chest. His arms slipped around her waist and she swayed toward him, crushed against him as his mouth came down to meet hers in a no-nonsense fashion, to part her lips and take possession.

She was lost in a giddying spiral of desire. His kisses were wonderful. A faint smell of a pine forest tempted her, and she ran her hands across broad, firm shoulders.

Something thumped on the other side of the door and they heard Kent say, "Kissie, kissie!"

Clarice laughed with Grady. "We have a date tomorrow night?" he asked.

"Yes," she answered eagerly, and he felt a flash of excitement and relief at the same time.

"And a date Saturday night?" he asked, holding his breath.

"Sorry, I have a date then with Sam. Now, you move out of my way and let's get back to work before Kent yells something worse than 'Kissie, kissie!' "

"I'll opt for giving Kent something to think about," Grady said, tightening his arms around her and bending over her. He molded her softness to his body as he kissed her hard, wanting her to faint from his kisses, wanting her to return them.

Return them she did, and he realized he'd better stop or they would be in real trouble. He straightened up, releasing her. She looked as dazed as he felt, and he wanted with every fiber of his being to pull her back into his arms. Her hair ribbon was askew and he smiled, tugging it free.

"Grady!" she said, but she wasn't indignant. The drawled word made his pulse jump another notch.

"Your ribbon was crooked."

"So's my blouse. Will you get to work! I'll never hear the end of this from Kent."

"I suppose you told Uncle Stanton I set fire to the kitchen."

"Yes, I had to."

"I know you did. Did you tell him why?"

"Well, I didn't tell him you were thinking about me and Sam," she said, straightening her blouse and smoothing it over her soft breasts. She reached up to catch her hair and tie it at her nape again.

didn't ask questions about his past, yet couldn't resist. "Where did you grow up?" she asked him, thinking Grady's eyes were often as deep green as the oak leaves on his lot. She was curious about his life before she had known him, feeling a deep urge to know him better.

"In Fort Worth, Texas," he said, reaching out to run his blunt fingers along his tall glass of iced tea. "Then we moved to Hot Springs, Arkansas, and when I was in high school we moved to Oklahoma City. Dad was manager in a chain of stores—Bixby Variety stores."

"Do you have any brothers or sisters?" she asked, listening and studying him at the same time.

"Yes, an older brother, Pat, who is married and lives in Houston." He stretched his arm across the table and touched the thin gold bracelet on her wrist. His fingertips were cold from resting on the icy glass. "Pat and Alice have two children, so I'm an uncle."

"Do you live in an apartment?" she asked.

"Mmm. Didn't you tell me your parents live in Tulsa?" he asked, changing the subject.

She knew it. He was hiding where he lived. "My father works for the Stone Brothers Paper and Box Company. Where's your father?"

"He's no longer living."

"I'm sorry. Does your mother work?"

"No." He circled her wrist lightly with his thumb and forefinger. "Delicate. You look fragile some-times, but you're not."

His eyes conveyed the rest of his message and she drew a deep breath, twisting her hand to slip her fingers through his. He smiled and she smiled in return, a silent exchange that reinforced the touching of hands.

When conversation resumed they pursued less personal topics, and she found that they were in agreement on major issues in the world. They even liked the same movies.

When they left the restaurant Grady drove through town and they looked at the new buildings along the west freeway. They stopped and had ice cream cones before he took Clarice home. Aware it was still early in the evening, she turned to him. "Would you like to come in?"

"I sure would," he said, and opened her door for her. Inside her small apartment he paused to look around. They were standing in a narrow entryway with a tile floor and white walls. Clarice tried to see the living room through his eyes as she glanced at the familiar beige furniture, brown rug, over-stuffed armchairs that were hand-me-downs, and chrome director's chairs. Plants hung in the windows and one wall had a painting of a stream, which she inherited from the previous tenant.

"How nice," he said.

"It's sort of plain."

He smiled at her. "It's yours and I like it."

"Want to listen to some music?"

"Sure." He followed her across the room and stood with his shoulder touching hers while she looked through her records.

He kissed the nape of her neck and she paused, holding a record in her hands.

"Grady . . ."

"I've wanted to kiss you since the moment I first saw you tonight." He turned her around and his arms slipped about her as he kissed her on the lips.

Clarice linked her arms around his neck, clinging to him, her thoughts as blank as a cloudless sky. She pressed against him, relishing his hard body, delirium rushing through her. It no longer mattered if he lived under a bridge or changed jobs constantly. She knew she was lost. For better or worse she was falling in love with Grady O'Toole, and she didn't see any way to prevent it.

His hand slid up, caressing the fullness of her breast, his fingers finding the nipple. She gasped with pleasure, and her hands slipped down his back, over firm buttocks to his thighs.

"Don't rush me," she whispered.

"I can't stop thinking about you," he said, his voice becoming gruff as it deepened. "I want you."

She was on fire and a last, faint shred of wisdom told her to take care. He was a man who took life in a casual manner, a man who might disappear from her life tomorrow. She pushed away, finding it more difficult than she would have imagined. His lips were red from kisses, his eyes half-closed, his breathing heavy. When she looked at him she wanted to pull him close again.

"I'm old-fashioned, Grady. You already know I can't take anything too lightly, especially a relationship with a man."

"Yeah," he said while his Voice of Reason told him he had just had a narrow escape.

"Maybe we should call it a night."

"Not yet. Put on the record and we'll talk."

He was true to his word, and they sat and talked

until after midnight. She lost track of time and was surprised when he stood up to go.

All the time they had talked she had wanted to be back in his arms. He had constantly touched her, little touches on her arm or shoulder, touches that from someone else would have been impersonal, but from Grady were incendiary.

He kissed her good night at the door and left, closing the door behind him. She leaned against it with her eyes closed, her heart pounding from his kiss.

"I don't want to be in love with a tamale vendor," she said to the empty hallway, and sighed. "I'm in love with a tamale vendor!" How could she explain it to her solemn, practical father, who had taught her that security should always come first in life?

While Clarice warred with her feelings, Grady suffered the same conflict. He drove home muttering to himself, his libido telling him it had been one of the best evenings of his life and how wonderful Clarice was, while his Voice of Reason said he was headed for more trouble than he had ever known.

Their Sunday date only intensified their feelings, and after that Clarice had no more dates with Sam. Every night after work she went out with Grady, on weekends, whatever night he wasn't working. And they never went to his place.

She asked him four times to return the job application form, and when he finally did she went right to her office, closed the door and read it swiftly. "Name: Grady O'Toole. Address: 33300 Wilmington."

She lowered the paper, frowning—she hadn't heard of a street called Wilmington.

She raised the paper again to read. "Phone: 555-0130. References: Sam Banks, Leonard Smith, T. Eliott." The spaces for phone numbers beside the three names were blank. She rushed across the room, picked up a city directory, and looked at a map to see where Wilmington Street was located.

That evening after work she drove to the address on the application. Wilmington was across the city and the house number Grady had given was a field of high green weeds between two concrete block warehouses. She stared at the field in consternation and wondered where Grady O'Toole slept at night.

Three more weeks passed while they dated, going out to eat or to shows, then back to her apartment, where they talked and kissed until Grady would go home.

Finally a night came when Clarice decided it was time she saw where he lived, whether it was under a bridge or not.

Eight

Grady turned the car toward her apartment, and Clarice shifted in the seat, idly tucking a strand of hair back in place where it was looped and pinned on top of her head. Her white V-necked blouse was tucked into her yellow cotton skirt, and she smoothed the skirt over her knees while she looked at him.

Grady's pale green shirt was open at the throat and his tan slacks fit his slender hips disconcertingly well. Her heartbeat speeded up. She wanted to touch him, to feel his arms around her. "Grady, let's go to your place tonight. I haven't seen where you live."

"Sure, but it's just a place where I live."

"It's part of you and I don't have any idea what it looks like. I want to see it."

He stared straight ahead as he drove, his features impassive, and she wondered what was running through his mind.

"Before we do," he said, "let's stop at your apartment and get a couple of your records."

She agreed, and within minutes she was unlocking her front door. Light spilled from the liv-

ing room, giving a faint illumination to the entryway. As she reached for the hall light switch, Grady's hand caught hers, his warm fingers wrapping
around hers to pull her gently into his arms.

"Grady . . ."

His lips stopped her words, his hands sliding up
her back to tangle in her hair while he kissed her.
Every night their kisses had been like kindling,
stacked bit by bit, until now his kiss started a con-
flagration. She trembled with need, her purpose in
coming home forgotten, only one thing on her
mind—Grady.

She loved him and wanted him desperately, and
all the wisdom in the world couldn't be heard over
her pounding heart. She felt complete in Grady's
arms. Life was happier, infinitely more exciting,
because Grady was so much that she was not. He
made her relax and laugh, made her look at life in a
more carefree manner, made her see redbirds and
oaks.

They kissed in the dimly lit hallway, and the
moment came when they always stopped. But
tonight when she tried to slip away, his arms tightened and he whispered, "Clarice, I love you. . . ."

Her heart thudded at his declaration, and she
wondered if he gave it as lightly as he dealt with
everything else is his life. For a moment some deep
instinct and years of training made her hesitate,
knowing that when she made a commitment it
would be deep and lasting.

"Clarice," he whispered again, his voice a caress.

"We're so different."

"I want you to let your hair down," he said in a
deep voice, his heavy-lidded gaze making her heart
pound wildly. She knew what he was asking—he

wanted more than her hair falling free. She knew he wanted the last barriers she kept between them to go down. And if she did what he asked, would she lose her heart forever?

He smiled faintly, his eyes devouring her until she trembled, but she reached up and slowly pulled a pin free, letting a lock of black hair tumble to her shoulders. His smile vanished and his breathing stopped momentarily. Time seemed suspended. Every glance, each touch, became permanently recorded in her memory. She pulled free another pin, hearing his hissing intake of breath.

Another long curl of raven hair fell on her shoulder. He reached out, catching it in his hand to tug gently.

"I'll finish," he whispered, pulling out a pin, and she knew she had made an irrevocable choice, one that might change her life. She wanted to give of herself as much as possible, to share intimacy with him, to bond the friendship and appease the hunger that seemed to grow each time they were together.

Her hair finally cascaded over her shoulders, and she was trembling from the effort to wait for Grady to touch and look and give his love the way he wanted.

His fingers fumbled the buttons free on her white blouse, pushing aside cotton and white lace to find her breast, and trace a dusty-pink nipple. The caress was ecstasy; the look on his face fanned flames that consumed her. She closed her eyes, clinging to him, her hands stroking him, love unfolding within her and blossoming like a flower opening to the sun while his tongue and hands traced patterns on her flesh.

He paused to unbutton his shirt, watching her with smoldering eyes that made her tremble. His broad bare chest was marvelous, and she reached for him, wanting to press against him and hold him. In moments he pushed away the rest of her clothing and held her away from him to look at her.

"In a hundred years," he whispered, "I don't think I could ever get tired of looking at you!"

When she looked at him she felt the same way. He was virile, strong, and fit—precious to her. She tugged at his belt, her fingers shaking with haste, and he helped her push his trousers to the floor. Them he picked her up and carried her to the bedroom while she locked her arms around his neck and kissed his throat.

He lowered her to the high four-poster and sank down, pulling her into his arms to stroke and caress her. He kissed her slowly, taking his time, watching her through lowered lids, his eyes as dark as emeralds. Her nerves singed with each touch, passion stirring her to reach for him. "Grady, I want you, I love you . . ."

He leaned over her, framing her face with his hands. "Tell me again, Clarice," he whispered, looking at her solemnly.

"I want you, and I love you."

Something flickered in the depths of his eyes before he crushed her to him, and patience and languor vanished.

His kisses were demanding, his caresses scorching as desire built, until he shifted her legs apart and moved between them. Lowering his weight, he entered her soft warmth.

When she cried out he hesitated a moment. "I don't want to hurt you," he said, his voice hoarse.

"Grady, come here," she urged, clinging to him. As her hips rose to meet him in an age-old dance, their hearts pounded in unison and she knew this was what she wanted. Whether her heart was wise or foolish, Grady was more important to her than anyone else on earth.

Her cry of ecstasy mingled with the words of endearment Grady whispered into her ear. "I love you, Clarice, I love you. . . ."

Then his words were gone as he gasped, and his body shuddered with release. When he lowered his full weight onto her she clung to him blissfully. Her thoughts were blank except for one thing—she was Grady's and at this moment he was hers.

He kissed her shoulder, her temple, pushing away damp strands of hair from her cheek. Then he rolled on his side and looked at her with a smile. "Happy?"

"Sublime," she said, and wound her arms around his neck. "I love you."

He smiled and leaned down to kiss the hollow between her neck and shoulder.

"Old-fashioned Clarice, who isn't old-fashioned in bed," he whispered, his lips against her flesh.

She laughed and ran her fingers over his bristly jaw, saying breathlessly, "Sexy Grady, who *is* sexy in bed!"

"I like to hear you laugh." He tickled her lightly and she laughed again, wriggling against him.

"Grady! It bothers you that I'm old-fashioned, doesn't it?"

"Nope, because it's just the right amount. It's a little quaint and—"

"Quaint!"

"Wonderful," he said quickly. "You're not too old-fashioned."

"That's good. I guess I'm just naturally that way. My family's a bit conservative." She ran her fingers over his chest. "You have a marvelous chest. I'll have to confess—that's why I missed the drive that morning—I was looking at your chest."

He chuckled and nuzzled her neck. "Am I still a tamale type?"

"Sorry. Will I ever hear the end of that?"

"I'm willing to forget it if you are."

She gazed into his eyes and the amusement faded from his face. Suddenly he was looking at her hungrily and his breathing deepened. "Clarice, I need you."

He leaned down, his arm tightening around her and his mouth covering hers, stopping the words she had been about to say, that she needed him more than he could ever guess. He was the sun in her life, and she clung to him, wanting to give him pleasure.

It was almost two in the morning when Grady dressed and left her after long kisses at the door. She locked the door behind him and returned to her room, staring at the mahogany bed, with its pink sheets, her simple old mahogany chest of drawers and dresser, feeling Grady's masculine aura still hovering in the room. She realized she had made a deep commitment during the evening. She also realized that she still hadn't seen where Grady lived.

At nine the next morning Grady turned in the long drive to King's Crown, passing his abandoned tamale cart. Morning sun filtered between the trees. The quiet surface of the lake was a silvery sheen, and the swans were puffs of white dotting the sloping green banks as they preened their feathers.

Feeling a deep-rooted contentment and thinking of Clarice, Grady hummed a tune. He tried to shut the future out of his thoughts, aware he was on thin ice in his relationship with her. She knew so little about him, and he wondered how she would take it when she discovered the truth. He glanced at King's Crown and stopped humming. The days at the restaurant were beginning to grate on his nerves. If it weren't for Clarice's presence, he would quit the job, but with her there . . .

Lost in memories of Clarice, he rounded the corner and saw Theo hoeing a small patch of ground at the edge of the parking lot. Sunshine caught auburn glints in his brown curls. He was wearing baggy plaid slacks, with a brown shirt and brown suspenders, looking as old-fashioned as a character from a long-ago movie.

Grady wondered vaguely what Theo was doing, but he had learned not to question Theo's actions.

When Grady parked and stepped out of his car, Theo smiled and leaned on his hoe. "Good morning. Isn't this a lovely day?"

Grady took a deep breath of fresh air and smiled. "It's grand."

"You don't see much sunshine in the restaurant."

"No, as a matter of fact, I don't."

"Don't you miss your tamale business just a little?"

Grady rubbed his hand across the back of his neck and stared at the tamale stand. "I haven't given it much thought." He continued to stare at the white tamale cart, weighing the two jobs in his mind. "Guess now that you mention it, I do miss it."

"Your tamales were good. You seemed to do a nice little business. Of course, I don't really know— this may be better. More lucrative perhaps."

"Hardly," Grady said dryly. "I earned more with my tamale stand."

"Did you now? Why'd you give it up? Security?"

"No, I thought this might be good experience."

"Oh, I see," Theo said, and began to hoe again.

Grady stared at the tamale stand. He had a glimmer of an idea about how the restaurant was run, he was still doing a menial task, and he could hardly concentrate whenever Clarice was around. In short, he realized, he was getting nowhere. Whereas, with the tamale stand . . .

He looked at Theo, who glanced up and smiled at him. "Listen to the redbirds," Theo said.

"Yeah."

"I suppose all you hear in the kitchen is the clatter of dishes. You should step outside every once in a while and listen . . . such a cheerful sound. Rather carefree. But then, I guess all birds are carefree."

"Are you trying to get me to quit work and go back to tamales?"

"Who, me?" Theo asked, his blue eyes wide and as innocent as the redbird's call. "I haven't said a word about your going back to it. I know this is secure and you're with Clarice all day. You're inside. You don't have to worry about a rainy day or snow. What had you planned to do about your tamales when it snows?"

"I'd worked that out. I was going to get a tent or something." Grady rubbed the back of his neck again.

"Well, there are so many other things—no security."

"I don't really give a damn about the security of washing dishes," Grady said mildly, looking at the tamale stand.

"Of course, you're with Clarice all day long."

"*And* I can't think straight when I'm with her," Grady admitted ruefully. Theo smiled at him.

"You're learning the restaurant business."

"Yeah, but I've reached a point now where I don't believe I'm going to learn much more unless Clarice gives me more management responsibility."

"Well, you must have some good reason for staying."

Grady stared at Theo a moment. He smiled and bent over the hoe. As Theo worked, Grady remembered how his tamale sales had been steadily increasing.

"Of course," Theo went on, "if you go back to it now, you'd have to start all over again building up business."

"I don't think so," Grady said. "I've been working here a month, but the tamale business was going well. I was on the verge of putting two or three more tamale stands around the city."

"My goodness, it certainly must have been going well!" Theo exclaimed, and paused with his arms on the top of the long wooden hoe handle. "You like working for yourself?"

"Yeah. I used to before I got the tamale stand. I haven't told Clarice yet what I used to do."

"Scared it will make a difference in her feelings for you?"

"No. I was more afraid of just the opposite. I wanted her to like me as a tamale vendor."

Theo laughed, his blue eyes sparkling. "I think you can set your mind at rest. What did you do before?"

"I was in the drilling business, but I haven't told her."

"Mum's the word. I'll wait and let you break the news. Drilling—and now tamales. Quite a change."

"Yeah, but I like it." Grady stared at Theo, who had gone back to hoeing a small patch of ground diligently. "What are you doing?"

"I thought the ground needed a little cultivation." Theo smiled. "I like to hear redbirds every now and then."

"I get the feeling I'm being manipulated."

"By Clarice?"

"No, not by her. Why did you tell the men to dump the dirt at the door of the restaurant?"

Theo paused. "I'm sorry. I don't know what you're talking about. What dirt?"

"You remember, last month the truckload of dirt that was dumped at the back door."

Theo scratched his head, jiggling his thick brown curls as he stared at the restaurant. "Dirt . . . I'm sorry. My memory is getting terrible. You know, I can remember what a loaf of bread cost twenty years ago, but I can't remember what I spent on groceries yesterday. You'll see how it is when you get older."

"Yeah," Grady said, and went inside, knowing it was futile to question Theo. He started washing heads of lettuce, staring out the window at Theo, who continued to hoe the same small patch of ground. Then his gaze shifted to the tamale stand, and the feeling that he should get back to tamales began to grow.

By the time he saw Clarice park and climb out of her car, he had made a decision. The skirt of her pink sundress swirled against her long, tanned legs as she came across the parking lot. A pink ribbon was tied around her black hair, and Grady's heart beat fast just at the sight of her. A momentary, fleeting argument rose that he would be happier working with her, but his Voice of Reason squelched it soundly.

When she came inside he asked her to step into the office a moment. The instant the door closed behind them he pulled her into his arms, inhaling deeply the sweet scent she always wore.

"Grady! We're at work."

"Hmmm," he said, nuzzling her neck. "You smell delicious."

"So do you," she answered breathlessly, moving her lips to meet his.

Sometime later she wriggled away and walked around the table she used as a desk to sit down facing him. He stood with his feet slightly apart, arms folded over his chest. His white cotton shirt was open at the throat and his dark slacks fit to perfection. She realized she was staring and asked, "You wanted to see me?"

"I sure did," he said, smiling at her.

"Well, there must have been more reasons than just to kiss."

"That's a dandy reason," he said, enjoying himself.

"Grady, will you be serious? If that's all . . ."

He waited with folded arms. She stared at him for a moment, then laughed. "That's all you wanted—to kiss me?"

He crossed the tiny room and reached down to pull her to her feet. "Grady, Kent will start something about us disappearing into my office. . . ."

"So what? You know what, Clarice? You laugh more than you used to."

"That's because of you," she said. Her voice had lowered and become breathless. She looked up at him, slipping her arms around him. She'd worry about Kent in a minute. Right now she wanted to kiss Grady and be kissed back.

How much time passed, she didn't know, but finally she leaned away slightly. "We have to go to work."

"I know. We have a date tonight."

"Yes."

"Hon, this has been wonderful. . . ." He paused to kiss her neck. "But I'm quitting. I'll give you only a week's notice because you can replace me with so little trouble."

"Mmm," she murmured, lost in his kisses until the words slowly penetrated her consciousness. She looked at him in shock. "You quit?"

"Yeah," he said, and kissed her ear.

"Grady!" She stepped back and stared at him, her hands on her hips. "You can't quit!"

"Why can't I?"

"Well, of course you can, but I thought . . . You and I . . . It's nice to work together."

"It's grand, but I'm not getting anywhere, Clarice."

"And you'll get somewhere with a tamale stand?"

"Yeah, I think so," he said, beginning to feel defensive.

Experiencing a mixture of emotions—disappointment, surprise, a slight annoyance—Clarice said, "Uncle Stanton isn't going to like this. He'll tell me to offer you a raise."

"Sorry, I won't take it."

"It'll be a big raise. He'd do most anything to keep you on."

"My mind's made up," he stated firmly.

She tilted her head to study him. "You have more future here than with a tamale stand."

"I don't think so. My tamale business was going great when I came to work here."

"How could it? It's just a little stand with tamales. You could work up here to assistant manager someday."

"It would take too long. Besides, I like being my own boss."

"You mean you don't really like to work."

"It's work just the same as this. Is my career going to come between us?" he asked lightly, but she had the feeling he was watching her closely.

"I hope not," she said, unable to give him a better answer. It disturbed her to think of him as a tamale vendor. "It just seems so . . . ambitionless, if there is such a word."

"It's carefree. It's a nice little business and I run it to suit myself." He smiled at her and suddenly she smiled in return.

"I'm going to miss you," she said, feeling it was a colossal understatement.

"I won't be far away," he replied. "And now, while we still work together . . ." His arms banded her waist, pulling her close to kiss her again.

"Clarice loves Grady! Whoopie, whoopie!" came from the other side of the door, and she stepped out of Grady's arms.

"I've got to stop him," she said.

"Sure," Grady said, and smiled at her as she opened the hall door. Kent disappeared into the dining room and Grady passed her to go back to work.

She stared at his broad back and sighed. It had been nice to work with him, and the restaurant wouldn't be the same. She couldn't see how a tamale stand would offer more for the future than working for a reputable, established restaurant, and Grady was good. He was efficient and could make quick, constructive decisions whenever the occasion arose. She frowned when she remembered she still didn't know where he lived—if it was out of his car or not. That worry was replaced with another one. Now she had to call Uncle Stanton and break the news about Grady's resignation.

She worked until the others had gone home. Grady waited with her to lock up, and while he swept the kitchen she called Uncle Stanton, who was now recuperating at home.

The moment he heard about Grady's resignation he began a blustery swearing. She held the phone away from her ear until he calmed.

"Well, I can get back to work next week," Uncle Stanton said. "I'll come down there tomorrow and see for myself how things are going. Offer him—dang blast it! Offer him a dollar more an hour."

"I'll make the offer, but I don't think anything short of making him manager will do."

"A tamale vendor can't run my restaurant! A dollar an hour. No more. I'll think of some way to get his tamale cart away from my place."

"I'll have the register receipts for you in the morning."

"You do that. I'll think about my next line of attack. In the meantime, you make him an offer."

"Yes, sir. 'Night, Uncle Stanton."

" 'Night."

She replaced the receiver, staring at the phone. "Trouble?" a deep voice asked, and she turned to find Grady standing in the open doorway.

"He said to offer you a dollar more an hour."

"Sorry. I need to get back to my tamale stand."

"I thought that's what you'd say. Shall we lock up and go?"

"Yeah, the sooner the better." He put his arm around her and together they walked out to the car.

As he drove down the drive she placed her hand on his arm. "Grady, I want to see where you live."

Nine

"I guess it's about time you did," Grady said, glancing at Clarice quickly.

She braced herself for the worst, noticing that he became pensive as he drove.

"Clarice, there are some things I need to tell you about myself."

Inwardly she cringed, fearing that his situation must be worse than she had imagined.

She waited, but he said nothing more, and she remained just as silent, wanting him to tell her in his own way and his own time. She noticed the neighborhood was becoming better as he drove. And it went from better to best, to one of the fine new residential sections of the city, where he turned into the drive of Windemere West Condominiums, elegant condos that were only a few years old.

Grady parked in a carport, helped her out, and they entered an enclosed patio that held clay pots of golden hibiscus and red geraniums. He unlocked the back door and led her inside.

"This is yours?" she asked, stunned at the elegance.

"Yes," he said, his eyes narrowed.

"I thought . . ." Her voice trailed away as she looked around at the lovely oak cabinets, an oval oak table and chairs, a tall yellow refrigerator-freezer, a microwave on the countertop. "You let me think . . ." She looked up at him, realizing how intently he was watching her. "I didn't think you had a home," she said quietly. "I pictured you living under a bridge. You have all this. . . ."

Suddenly he laughed, startling her. "Under a bridge?" He reached for her. His warm hands rested on her bare shoulder and he ran one finger across the strap of her sundress, but for once she wasn't totally distracted. "You sound angry."

"Well, you gave me another impression entirely. Why?"

He slipped his arms around her. She stood stiffly, seeing amusement and something else, something undefinable, dance in his eyes. With his first words she realized he was happy and relieved.

"Hon, I wanted you to love me whether I was a tamale vendor or not," he said gently. "I never under any circumstances thought you would be angry to find out that I had more than a nickel to my name."

"You haven't been honest with me!"

"I know I haven't and I'm sorry, but I wanted you to love me no matter what I had."

She stared at him, realizing how strongly he felt about the situation. "I do," she said, knowing her feelings for him ran deeper than she wanted to explore. Curiosity about him grew swiftly. "How do you know Sam Banks?"

"He used to work for me," Grady answered, taking her hand. "Let's go sit down and I'll tell you about my past. Want something to drink? Tea? Coffee?"

"I'll take a glass of iced tea."

"Sure thing." He moved swiftly around the kitchen, pouring two glasses of tea from a pitcher in the refrigerator. "C'mon," he said. "Let's sit in the living room."

For a moment she felt awed by the beautiful pale blue upholstery on the furniture, the antiques that decorated the room, the stately grandfather clock, and the oil paintings on the walls. Grady sank down on the sofa and pulled her down beside him.

"What do you want to know?"

"Everything. Why are you selling tamales?"

"Let me start back a few years," he said, trailing his fingers along her knee. A tingle caught part of her attention. "I have a degree in engineering, and when I was twenty-six I started my own drilling business. It grew and the oil boom helped. Three years ago my cousin Bart wanted to work with me and came into the business. He's good at working with people; I'm good out in the field. The business grew and we expanded. He put up some money and I made him a partner. Mom is an officer in the corporation, and we gave her some of the stock.

"My cousin Bart is an aggressive man and he wanted the whole business to himself. He offered once to buy me out and I told him I didn't want to sell. I offered to buy him out so he could start his own business. He rejected the offer, because he didn't want to go back to a smaller business. We argued about it for a while. Later he went behind my back, talked Mom into selling some of her shares to him, and eventually he owned controlling interest and wanted to buy me out."

"Didn't your mother know what he was doing?"

"No. She's never worked and she doesn't pay much attention to what goes on in our company."

"So you sold your business?"

"No. We're working it out. In the meantime I'm out of it and that's when I happened on the tamale cart."

She laughed, shaking her head. "From engineering to tamales! Grady, that's impossible!"

"I saw that stand for sale and suddenly I just bought it. I'd spent about two weeks sitting around here getting more nervous by the minute, when I saw the tamale cart. It's been grand. I told you, I like redbirds and oaks. I like the challenge of it."

"So you'll take life easy with the tamale stand?" she asked, trying to keep disappointment out of her voice.

"I don't know. It may be temporary, it may not be."

"Grady. it's so . . . so casual. There are no benefits, no retirement or insurance or hospitalization."

He grinned. "Practical, cautious Clarice. If I build it up to a certain level, I can get those things. Right now I'm willing to take the risk to be my own boss rather than opt for security and insurance."

"Time goes in a hurry, Grady, and you can't get it back," she said, appalled at his attitude, at discovering a gulf between them bigger than she had suspected. "Three years from now you'll still be standing out with the birds and trees and you won't have much more than you do now."

"Maybe, maybe not," he said quietly, but she detected a note of steel. "I don't know what I'll be doing three years from now. I'm suing Bart for the business—"

"You're *what*?"

"I'm suing him. I'm not giving up without a fight. I started that business and I'm entitled to more than he plans to give me."

"You're suing your relative?"

"Uh-oh. That tone of voice means you don't approve."

She stared at him, realizing how little she knew him, and how much she had misjudged him. "Well, I'm shocked," she said cautiously.

"Why?"

"That's rather harsh. I can't imagine suing one of my relatives," she said, but that wasn't what bothered her the most. He waited and she tried to put her feelings into words. "You're not what I thought. You're hard and ambitious—a different man than I thought I knew."

"Not really. Maybe you had the wrong impression because of the tamale stand, but I'm still me—Grady O'Toole."

"How can you sue a relative?"

"He did it to me first, remember? He took my company right out from under me," Grady said tensely, his dark brows drawing together in a frown.

"Even so, how can you go to court to get it back? I couldn't do that to a relative."

"You don't know until you're in a situation like I'm in. There's a sizable amount of money involved."

"That isn't as important as family ties."

"It is to me and my cousin," he said, trailing his fingers above her knee. "Is this going to come between us?" he asked lightly, then looked up at her when she didn't answer.

"I don't understand you," she said. "I don't understand how you can sue your cousin. I don't understand why an engineer would get a tamale stand and open a little business when you could go right out and get a job in your profession."

"After having my own business it's difficult to adjust to working for someone. And I got the tamale stand as a lark, to help pass time while I waited for the lawsuit to come up. Once I got into selling tamales, I found out I liked it."

He slipped his arm around her waist and pulled her onto his lap. "One thing I know, I'm still very much in love," he said. He leaned down to kiss her, his thick lashes lowering as he closed his eyes. She slid her arms around his neck and raised her lips, taking his kiss, but deep down something had changed in her feelings for him. She was shocked and slightly awed to discover what he was really like underneath the easygoing charm. Gradually, though, her worries melted away as Grady's caresses took her full attention and his murmured endearments brought warmth back into the room.

It was after one in the morning when he took her home and kissed her good night. Clarice closed the door behind him, then walked into her bedroom, in shock over all she had learned about Grady.

Another cold thought gripped her—she knew their relationship wasn't permanent. She realized while Grady declared he loved her, he had no intention of making a deep commitment with his life as unsettled as it was at present.

With this disturbing fact she climbed into bed to stay awake for another hour. The next morning she drove to work and a block away saw the "O'Toole's Hot Tamales, Yum-Yum!" sign fluttering in the breeze. And there was Grady, back in cut-offs, the sight of his marvelous chest tugging at her senses. When she waved and smiled he waved and smiled back.

The moment she stepped into King's Crown she was met at the door by a scowling Kent.

"Watch out, Sis. He's back."

"Who's back?"

"Uncle Stanton. He's storming around here, dissatisfied with everything we've done."

"How can he be? Everything's better."

"Not to his way of thinking."

"Theo!" a gravelly voice snapped, and Kent jumped.

"Uh-oh! Here he comes." Kent disappeared into the kitchen as Uncle Stanton came around the corner from the dining room, a familiar sight in his gray sharkskin suit, the elbows and trousers shiny from years of wear.

"Where's Theo? He's as elusive as the wind!" Uncle Stanton muttered while he hobbled on a cane. His feet were in slippers with the toes cut out, and beneath neatly combed straight brown hair his forehead was wrinkled in a scowl.

"Clarice! It's ten minutes after ten. I thought you got here earlier."

"Usually I do."

"Come into my office and we'll have a little talk."

"Yes, sir." Uncle Stanton's office smelled faintly musty. Stacks of papers were everywhere, a glass-front bookcase was filled with old books, and hanging above a cluttered rolltop desk was a year-old calendar.

Uncle Stanton sat down in a swivel chair and propped his feet on a cardboard box. "We need to go over a few things. The fruit bill is high this past week."

"The price of fruit has gone up. I'm buying at the same place you always have."

"Then you should've shopped around when the price went up. There have been some changes in the menu."

"I did that. Cuong told me about some recipes he's tried and one of them was my idea. We can get fresh fish at a reasonable price now, so I added it and it seems to be popular. Cuong's talents are marvelous with seafood."

"Humpf. Too many items run up a bigger overhead. This has been an excellent steak house for years."

"Fish is becoming very popular now that we can get it fresh here in the Midwest. There's a central market that has it flown in daily."

"I know that, but the more items you offer, the more headaches you have in the kitchen. Need to keep expenses down. I'll take over the bar."

"What will Uncle Theo do?" she asked, shocked.

Uncle Stanton's dark eyes shifted to an old picture on the wall of a tiny lunchroom that had been his first venture into the restaurant business. Clarice dreaded hearing his answer. "Theo can go back to the fence business," he said.

"But you said if business increased—"

"It hasn't increased enough and I have big bills. I have to cut back. Times are getting harder."

"That isn't what you promised us," she said, unable to believe she was hearing right.

"I have to do what I have to do. I'm making you manager and you can continue as you have. I can't give the percentages that I promised, because the expenses are high and I'm afraid we're heading into a tough fall."

She listened in dismay, stunned that he would go back on his word.

"Kent will have to go," Uncle Stanton continued, "but he was going anyway. This will only be a week or two sooner."

"I'd rather you kept Uncle Theo than me," she said. "I can go back to my old job."

"Nope. Need a pretty gal to seat people, and I can take care of the bar."

"The bar receipts have increased the most," she said. "Eight percent, whereas the rest of the business is showing a five-percent increase. That's because of Uncle Theo. People like to talk to him."

"Stuff and nonsense! They like to talk to anyone. I'll talk to them. I didn't build this restaurant up by ignoring customers. Now, you keep your nose to the grindstone and if we do enough business, I'll give you a raise."

"Yes, sir," she said perfunctorily, worrying about Uncle Theo. "Does Uncle Theo know?"

"Yes. He goes from job to job anyway. This release didn't raise his temperature. That's the way it has to be if I'm going to keep my head above water. Do you know how many restaurants went under in this city last month?"

"No, sir."

"Seven. That's a lot in a month's time."

"Yes, it is."

"I don't want to be a casualty, and there'll just have to be some tightening of the belt to make ends meet."

"Yes, sir."

"Well, let's get back to work."

She left his office in a state of shock and hunted for Uncle Theo. She found him outside. "Uncle Theo! I've been looking for you."

"I'm right here," he said, as cheerful as ever.

"I just talked with Uncle Stanton and he told me the news."

"Yes, so I'll be leaving at the end of this week."

"I'm so sorry."

"Not to worry your pretty head about it. I'm not worried. There's always a job somewhere," he said calmly. "Something new to discover, new people to meet."

"You sound like Grady. It won't be the same here without you."

"I'll be all right. You'll see. I'm not surprised. Stanton's just Stanton through and through. We better get inside. Lunch customers will start arriving soon."

She felt a little better after talking to him, but that night her tranquil feelings dissolved beneath Grady's scowling countenance.

He stood in the center of his living room, his hands on his jean-clad hips, his brown hair damp from a shower after work. His pale yellow knit shirt molded his powerful chest, but Clarice's attention was held by the fire in his eyes. "Your uncle won't live up to his promises!" Grady said heatedly.

"He said restaurants are facing harder times and he can't afford to give salary increases or keep Uncle Theo on the staff."

"What's Theo say about it?"

"He took it in stride, as he always does. Uncle Theo is the eternal optimist."

"Well, that's a raw deal."

"We're not going to sue," she said firmly, crossing her legs.

"My lawsuit still rubs you the wrong way."

"I just don't understand."

"I don't understand the three of you smilingly accepting your uncle Stanton's underhanded treatment!" Grady snapped. "He made you a deal—promised you certain things if you increased business. You increased business and he didn't keep his promises. You're letting him walk over you and Theo and Kent."

"It's his business and he can do as he chooses, remember?"

"Yeah, but a deal's a deal. You could protest what he's doing and stop accepting it with a smile."

"Maybe I'm more like Uncle Theo than I realized."

"Your Uncle Theo gets along."

"He barely has a penny. He never saves because he always gives away what he has to someone needy or to some cause."

"He still gets along. He's happy as a lark whatever he's doing. Whereas you're going to be miserable working with your uncle Stanton."

"How do you know that?" she asked in spite of similar thoughts she'd had on the subject.

"I know you. He's a narrow-minded, miserly grouch who will keep right on taking advantage of you as long as you let him."

"You don't know," she said, beginning to grow angry. "He has his good points. He's a good businessman, you'll have to admit."

"Yep, I'll agree to that. King's Crown is a fine restaurant. He knows the restaurant business, but I'll bet Cuong gets a better deal than you do, because he'll walk out if he doesn't."

His remark stung, because after running the restaurant in Uncle Stanton's absence, she knew that Cuong did, indeed, have a better deal.

"I'll bet Cuong gets a raise, too," Grady added.

"I don't think he will. Uncle Stanton said he had to tighten his belt, so to speak."

Grady sat down near her and leaned forward, his elbows on his knees. "I'll bet you Saturday night dinner that Cuong just got a raise."

"It's a deal!" she said heatedly, feeling upset and angry. "Whatever Uncle Stanton does, I'm not going to take him to court. He's my blood kin."

"Then you're either scared or—"

"Or what, Grady?" she asked impersonally, wondering what was happening between them and feeling a cold touch of fear that their personality differences were too great to surmount. "Is a dollar more important to you than family? What's the suit doing to the rest of your family? Aren't they taking sides? Isn't it dividing everyone?"

He looked startled and his face flushed. Grady stared at her in consternation. She was right about dividing his family, he thought. It was something he hated and had tried to overlook. As he stared at Clarice, he reminded himself that she was trouble in his life. At the same time he remembered the wonderful moments, her laughter that brightened the day, her interest and willingness to listen to his problems, the wild, passionate abandon. . . .

"You're right," he admitted, rubbing his hands

together as his thoughts changed from Clarice to his family. "Mom's sick about it. My aunt and uncle won't speak to me and are less than civil to Mom. But, dammit, I'm not going to hand over a business I built just because Bart wants to take it!"

He stood up and jammed his hands into his pockets to stride across the room. He didn't hear a sound, but in a few seconds her hands slipped around his waist from behind and she hugged him.

"Grady," she said so quietly he could barely hear her. "Let's go out to the park on the way to dinner and look at the oaks and redbirds."

He turned around, feeling his tension dissipate. He pulled her close, leaning down to kiss her. "Good idea," he whispered as his lips met hers.

They walked through the park, enjoying the green willows and blooming rose bushes, the quietness, but Clarice could feel the strain in him and she knew there was a wall between them that hadn't been there before.

During dinner they were careful to keep off the sensitive subjects of their families and careers. Later, when they were in her apartment and Grady pulled her into his arms, his kisses were hard and passionate. Once he turned his head to whisper into her ear, "I've found something special in you. I don't want to lose it."

"You won't," she said, framing his face in her hands, her pulse racing as she looked at the features that were so dear to her. Her gaze drifted down to the open V of his shirt, and she forgot differences and families and jobs as Grady's hand found her breast.

Clarice closed her eyes and gasped with pleasure, clinging to the man she knew she loved with all her heart.

For the next week they tried to skirt the volatile issues, carefully keeping their talk on neutral subjects, but gradually it began to be a strain to avoid topics and be cautious in their conversation.

Uncle Theo left the restaurant, Kent went back to a job at Hamburger Heaven, and one waitress quit and wasn't replaced. Uncle Stanton began giving Clarice more and more hours to work, getting her to type letters for him, little tasks that made Grady angry or solemn if she mentioned anything about them to him. She knew he was holding back what he really wanted to say to her about the situation.

One morning she was on an errand for Uncle Stanton, driving on South Boulevard toward the Farmer's Market. The four-lane express road was filled with swiftly moving cars. She had a green light at one intersection and sped along with the flow of traffic. She glanced idly at the vacant lot on the southeast corner of the intersection, and saw it was no longer empty. A white tamale cart stood there and a short man was turning tamales. A customer waited in front of the stand. The man's head was bent, a large Mexican hat hiding his face. Beside the stand was a fluttering banner that read, "O'Toole's Hot Tamales, Yum-Yum!"

She tried to glance in the rearview mirror as she passed the lot, but traffic was too busy. She knew Grady wasn't selling the tamales because he had been at his stand when she'd left the restaurant. He hadn't told her he was expanding, and she wondered how many tamale carts he had around the city.

She ran the errand, purchased the fresh pineapples Uncle Stanton had ordered, and started back to King's Crown. As she approached the busy corner again, she had another green light. She wanted to stop and look, but she had to keep moving. She glanced quickly to her left and received a shock. Uncle Theo was selling O'Toole's tamales!

Ten

"Oh, no!" she said grimly, clutching the steering wheel as she drove swiftly back to the restaurant. When she turned into the drive Grady was surrounded with cars and customers. She went into the restaurant and deposited the pineapples and the bill, then marched down the drive to Grady's tamale stand.

He was shirtless, wearing the sombrero, his feet in sandals, and her temper cooled a notch as she studied him. Looking at his burnished skin and his magnificent physique, her thoughts began to wander. Finally there was a lull in his business and she stepped closer, near an oak tree.

"Grady."

He turned around, a smile lighting his eyes. "Ah, you came to eat a tamale with me."

"No, I didn't."

"Oh? Something's wrong."

"How come you have Uncle Theo selling tamales?"

"I offered him a job and he accepted. It's honest work. Don't you think you should discuss this with *him*? He's capable of making his own decisions."

"He'll do it for you because he'll think he's helping you. He needs a job with security. At his age—"

"He's doing just what he wants. You talk to him about it."

"A tamale vendor. That's just revolting."

"That's what I am," Grady said coolly.

"There's no future in it."

He shrugged. "There's enough future to suit me. I started this at the beginning of the summer. Now I have three stands in the city."

"You do?" she asked, momentarily startled.

"Yes, as a matter of fact."

She stared at him, a mixture of feelings coursing through her. He walked over to her, and rested his hand on the tree behind her. Suddenly all she was aware of was Grady. His chest was almost touching her, the delicious scent of woods assailed her, and his muscled arm was inches from her cheek. She knew what it felt like to touch him, to be pressed against his chest, and she wanted to be held in his arms now. She ran her fingers along his arm. "You have a body that's terribly distracting. Muscles, and all that."

"Thank you, and the same to you. You smell nice," he said, breathing deeply. "You can eat a tamale with me. Have you had lunch?"

"No, I don't think so," she answered, not sure about the conversation. Grady looked at her lips and she couldn't breathe. He leaned a fraction closer and she had to close her eyes, to tilt her head up eagerly for his kiss.

His lips brushed hers, then settled on them, opening them, and he thrust his tongue against hers. She trembled with desire, on fire from the first touch. After a moment, though, she opened her eyes and leaned away from him slightly.

"Is what we have between us purely physical?" she asked.

"I don't think so," he answered, and his voice dropped, sounding gruff and slightly breathless. "I know there's more than physical attraction, but this is wonderful." He slipped his arm around her waist and kissed her until she wanted to fling her arms around him and forget the world.

A car honked and she pulled away, suddenly becoming practical. "We have to stop."

He grinned and unfolded a chair for her. "Sit down and let me serve you a tamale."

"I should get back to work. It's getting close to noon and this is a busy time at the restaurant."

"C'mon, Clarice, take a moment to enjoy life," he coaxed, smiling at her. "You work like a Trojan for your uncle."

Deciding to try life Grady's way, she sat on the ground, tucking her navy skirt around her legs. Grady filled two paper plates with steaming tamales and handed her one along with a plastic fork. He poured two paper cups of cool lemonade and sat down facing her.

No sooner had he sat down than a customer stopped and he had to get up again. While he worked, Clarice cut into the hot tamale and took a bite, closing her eyes as she relished the delicious taste. No argument that O'Toole's hot tamales were the best in town. Probably the best in any town! She finished hers while Grady waited on a steady stream of customers.

"Your tamales will be cold now," she said when he finally returned to her. "They're delicious."

"Thank you," he said, getting hot ones and sitting down to face her. "I'm doing pretty well with the stand. It's modest, but it's a start."

"I don't know how you can maintain your condo on a tamale stand."

"Well, to be honest, I can't. I'm in the red, but it's growing and that's what's important."

She looked into his eyes and saw how earnest he was. "It's growing so much you'd toss aside an engineering career?"

"I like the challenge. I think I can make a go of this. I'm looking for a building in a good location where the rent isn't too high to handle. I know I'll be in the red for a time, but I have savings."

"Oh, Grady, what a gamble!" she exclaimed, loving him, and at the same time hating the chance he was taking.

"I've projected what I'm doing. This business has jumped each week. What I'd like to do is open a small restaurant, try to keep the overhead down, and keep the stands around the city. Besides selling tamales at the stands and a small restaurant, I'd like to sell them to other restaurants as well."

"Other restaurants would buy from you?"

"I don't know why not if I make them a good deal. The product is fresh and wholesome, with no preservatives. It hasn't been frozen; it's very tasty." His eyes sparkled. "I'm going to ask your uncle if he'd like to buy some tamales for King's Crown."

She laughed, wanting to reach over and touch him, enjoying the sparkle in his eyes. "It sounds so risky."

"It is, but I've been amazed at how well business has gone with just this cart."

"That's true." She smiled at him. "Maybe they stop because of the body behind the cash register."

He grinned. "I don't think so. I get as many males as females. I'm just glad one certain female feels that way."

She winked, and he reached up to slip his hand behind her neck. "I like to talk to you about my plans. What about yours, Clarice? Do you always want to work at the restaurant?"

"I just want a secure job and something I like. I like orderliness and routine. I couldn't take the risk you're taking." Her gaze shifted from the oak leaves to Grady. "We're very different."

"Thank heavens!" he said. "I wouldn't fall in love with another me."

She laughed. "Maybe your plans will work."

"But you don't really think so?"

"I'd never dream of taking the chance, but that doesn't mean I don't think you'll succeed."

He smiled and she knew he was pleased, but she felt a chill of fear as she looked at him. He was starting a risky venture and one that might not leave a place in his life for her. She needed to see where she was going, and for once in her life she couldn't. She was at a loss when she thought about their relationship and the future.

"Why so solemn?" he asked.

It was on the tip of her tongue to tell him that she didn't think his future would include her, but she didn't want polite protests that were meaningless. And she didn't want to push him into a commitment he didn't want, so she smiled and kept quiet about her worries. "I just don't see how you can risk your savings on it when you have a safe alternative." She brushed off her skirt. "I better get back. Uncle Stanton will see me over here and have a fit."

"Yeah. He was over here yesterday with another offer to buy me out."

"There are other places in the city."

"I'm thinking about accepting this offer."

"You are?"

"It's a big hunk of money."

She was startled that Uncle Stanton had offered Grady something generous after all his talk about belt-tightening and hard times.

"What's the matter?" Grady asked. "You don't want me to take his offer?"

"Oh, no! You know what's best for you. I'm just surprised because he's talked about times getting tough and how he has to economize."

"Your uncle Stanton is going to economize exactly where he sees he can without hurting the business. He's doing a whale of a business and you know it. And it increased when you were there and changed the menu to include fish."

"This is old ground, Grady. And dangerous ground," she said, and stood up, smoothing her skirt and brushing grass off it.

"You owe me a dinner too," he said, standing up to face her, "because Cuong got a raise last week."

"He didn't!" A little flare of shock and anger ran through her.

"Oh, yes, he did. I talk to him every now and then. Cuong has developed a great craving for tamales. He gets them on his way home."

"Good grief!" she exclaimed, temporarily distracted. "He's one of the best cooks in town. He can eat what he wants at the restaurant."

"Doesn't your uncle charge you if you eat there?"

"Yes, otherwise everyone would eat into the profits."

"Sure," Grady said with a cynical note that cut.

"You don't agree with anything Uncle Stanton does!"

"Not the things that take advantage of his family and employees. He could give a discount."

"Grady, you're not one to talk about families!"

He felt his cheeks grow hot as he fought to control his temper. She bothered him with her remarks about his family, because he didn't like what was happening either, but it seemed necessary to fight for his rights.

"I better go," Clarice said stiffly, spots of color coming into her cheeks. Grady watched her walk away, her skirt pulling slightly across her hips in a provocative way with each step, her dark hair bouncing slightly between her shoulders. He hurt. He wanted her back, wanted to hear her laugh, ached to hold her. He knew his words had stung and bothered her just as much as hers had bothered him.

That night, when they sat across from each other at an Italian restaurant, Clarice said, "This weekend my folks are coming from Tulsa and I'd like them to meet you. I'm going to have a family dinner Friday night."

"Holy smoke." He placed his fork in his plate. "I forgot. Mom wants to meet you and I was going to ask you both to dinner this weekend. Let me take your family too."

"There's too many of us. Why don't you bring your mother? I'll call her and ask her."

"It won't be too many, and I want to take you out. Do I ask your uncle Stanton?"

"He won't leave the restaurant. I've already talked to him about it."

"I'll tell Theo and Kent," Grady said. He watched her closely as he added, "I might as well tell you now. Kent's coming to work for me."

"Oh, no! Grady, are you going to employ all my family running tamale stands?"

"Well, if they want the jobs, I don't see why not."

She stared at him in consternation. "When is Kent working? He isn't skipping school is he?"

"Nope. After school and on Saturdays and Sundays."

She sat back and laughed. "I give up! Next thing you'll offer *me* a job as a tamale vendor."

He grinned, his eyes suddenly beginning to sparkle. "Anytime. You just say the word and I'll set you up in business," he said, and his libido danced in circles. "Talk about traffic stopping for a body. If you'd wear a bikini . . ."

"Don't be ridiculous!" she said, and laughed.

"It's better when we agree on something. And it's much better when you're happy."

Her eyes clouded and he wished he hadn't brought up their disagreements. He reached across the table to touch her cheek. "Let's get out of here and go to my place."

She nodded and he stood up to take her arm, holding her close to him, feeling as if he needed her desperately.

*   *   *

That weekend Clarice bought a new dress for the family dinner, a simple navy one with a V neck and a straight skirt. She pinned her hair in a bun on top of her head and wore dangling thin gold earrings that jiggled when she moved. She felt a touch of nervousness over her parents meeting Grady and told herself it was ridiculous. Her nervousness vanished when she opened the door to greet Grady.

He was wearing a navy suit, a white shirt, and a dark tie, and was the most handsome man she had ever seen. He looked conservative, successful, and breathtaking. "My goodness!" she said, and he grinned.

"My goodness, yourself," he whispered. "Are your folks here?"

"No. They're waiting at Uncle Theo's. I told them we'd meet them. I'll take my car and you take yours."

"We can all ride in mine," he said, moving closer. "You look gorgeous. I think I'd rather stay right here." He stepped inside and closed the door, and her temperature jumped. Silently she agreed with him, but she knew five people were waiting for them.

"Mom and Dad said they'll drive and Kent will probably ride with them," she said.

"Is that right?" he asked politely, resting both hands on the wall on either side of her. "You have a new dress."

"Yes, just for you."

"It's great!" His eyes darkened and he leaned closer.

"Grady, we're supposed to be there now."

"Mmm. Clarice, shh." He leaned down to kiss her throat, beneath her ear, her cheek, and she had to turn her face, to touch his lips and kiss him.

His hands trailed down over her hips, pulling her close, and for a moment she relished his caresses.

"Grady, we have to stop."

"Why?" he whispered, his hand slipping beneath her low neckline.

She closed her eyes, trying to cling to wisdom and remember they were supposed to be somewhere. "Grady, we have to go."

"In a minute," he drawled, and the minute became minutes and then a quarter of an hour.

"Oh, my word, Grady, we're late!"

He grinned and ran his finger along her throat. "It was worth it. You know what I'd like to do?" he asked in a husky voice that caused a shower of hot sparks in her.

"Never mind. Now's not the time or place."

He laughed and hugged her. "How do you know what I have in mind?"

She wriggled away and tried to straighten her dress. Her cheeks were pink when she looked in the entryway mirror. He moved behind her, and she glanced at his image as he pressed against her. "You can't imagine," he whispered, leaning down to kiss the nape of her neck, "what you did to me that day the dirt caved in and I fell on top of you."

"I don't have to imagine," she said breathlessly, "I know. I was there, remember?"

He laughed softly. "Clarice, it can be so good between us." He looked at her reflection, and she knew he was thinking about their differences because he became solemn, staring at her intently.

Grady ached with desire. He wanted Clarice more than he had ever wanted a woman. He felt incomplete away from her. And he was torn with indecision for the first time in his life. He was accustomed to weighing facts and making a judgment and acting on it. Now he was in a quandary ninety percent of the time. Moments came when it was on the tip of his tongue to ask her to marry him. Then he'd think of all the risk he was taking, of her love of security, and he was afraid he'd lose her for good if he asked her.

She frowned, her blue eyes clouding with worry, and he knew she felt the same unsettling fears he did. They were different, and part of their differences might be too large to be surmounted. His Voice of Reason argued that now was no time to take on more responsibility, no time for deep commitments if he wanted to make a go of his business.

He pulled her to him roughly, crushing her as if he could hold her forever. She clung tightly to him, but somewhere deep inside he had a feeling of doom that he couldn't shake.

They drove to Grady's mother's home, a two-story brick and frame house in an older part of town. Grady took Clarice's arm when they stepped out of the car. "Come see where I grew up," he said.

"You said you moved around a bit."

"I did, but we moved here when I was in high school—too far ahead of you for you to know me, youngster that you are."

"My dear old man!" He grinned, and she looked around at a yard shaded with oaks, a swing on the wide porch. "Oh, Grady, it's so nice. Our house was plainer. Mom and Dad are very practical people. No frills at all."

"A little frilliness runs in your family somewhere. Theo has more than a fair share."

She laughed. "I know, but I'm warning you, my parents don't have much sense of humor."

"You and Kent do."

"Goodness, Kent's more like Uncle Theo than like Dad. I hope your mother likes me."

"She'll love you. She's so embarrassed over the tamale business, she'll hardly claim me."

"She is?"

"That surprises you?"

"Yes. Somehow I figured she's just like you."

"Nope. You'll see. I take after Dad."

Clarice did see the moment the door opened. The short plump woman facing them had dark hair and dark eyes and bore little resemblance to her son until she smiled. Her smile was warm and welcoming, and Clarice instantly felt a sense of relief.

"Come in," Mrs. O'Toole said.

"Mom, this is Clarice Jenkins. Clarice, my mother, Harriet."

"It's nice to meet you, Mrs. O'Toole."

She laughed and squeezed Clarice's hand. "Call me Harriet. Grady's told me about you. You're as pretty as he said. Grady, show her the house while I finish getting ready."

"Sure, Mom," he said, and dropped his arm around Clarice's shoulders. In a few minutes she knew where Grady got his love of antiques. In the spacious living room she saw ornate gilt mirrors, fragile china vases, a Dresden figurine, a Wedgwood pitcher, an Oriental rug with deep blue and red.

"Grady, what a lovely home."

"Want to see my room?" he drawled in a teasing leer, and she laughed.

"Of course. We have a chaperon."

"She loves you."

"She doesn't know me!"

"I can tell, though. She wouldn't have asked me to show you the house. Mom's old-fashioned—"

"Grady, if you call me old-fashioned one more time . . ." Clarice said, letting the threat hang unspoken in the air.

He laughed and squeezed her to him, dropping a kiss on her forehead. "I told you," he whispered into her ear, "you're never old-fashioned in bed."

"I may wait out in the car for you!"

"No, you won't. You want to see my room too much."

He was right. She was curious and wanted to know all about him. The room still looked like it belonged to a boy in high school, and trophies lined a bookshelf.

"My goodness! I'm impressed. Football and swimming. That's where you got . . ."

"Got what?" he asked, his eyes dancing while he waited. He tugged on her ear and laughed.

"Don't deny you're old-fashioned," he said. "It still makes you blush to talk about a man's body."

"Maybe so. I can't recall ever dating anyone where the subject came up with regularity."

"I'm glad to hear it."

She looked around. "I don't have a room to show you because my folks moved after I was away from home, but I can tell you, I didn't have an array of awards and trophies and honors."

"So what?" he asked with a smile that warmed her like sunshine. "I'm not going out with you because of old trophies. No, hon, you have other assets." His gaze lowered, and he drawled, "Yes, sir."

Teasing him in return, she put her hand at her waist and wiggled her hips. "You like my assets, huh?"

"Mmm!" He reached for her, but she backed away with a laugh. When she turned to look at the trophies he moved away, and she didn't realize what he was doing until she heard the door close behind her.

"Grady, what on earth?"

He crossed the room to take her into his arms, and she protested, "Your mother's here! You'll embarrass me."

"Give me just a kiss," he coaxed, and she obliged fully.

Minutes later she stared dazedly at him, seeing him look at her in the hungry way that made her pulse keep right on racing along.

"That's one of the things I like," he said. "You respond to me."

"Do I ever!" she said breathlessly.

"We're going to work things out," he said. "I need you."

She hoped to the depth of her being that he meant what he said. He stepped away, turning his back momentarily while his breathing became normal. She straightened her dress, glancing at herself in a small mirror over a tall maple chest of drawers. Her cheeks were pink, her lips red from

Grady's kisses, and her hair was slightly loosened, giving her a more casual look. She smoothed her hair and repinned a strand.

"Grady, you've got me tangled up."

When he didn't answer she glanced at him, and her heart jumped at the intense look in his eyes. He stared at her solemnly, his hands jammed into his pockets.

"I won't tell you what you've done to me," he said. "I've never been this way before in my life."

"How's that?"

From downstairs his mother called, "Grady!"

He shrugged. "We better go."

Clarice felt disappointment and curiosity, wanting to know what he had been about to say, but she knew his mother was waiting, and they were late.

"This is embarrassing." She smiled and took his arm, suddenly feeling giddy and happy as she winked at him. "But I loved it!"

He looked startled, then laughed and slipped his arm around her shoulders as they went downstairs.

Kent rode with them, and Theo rode with Clarice's parents. At the restaurant Grady had selected they were seated in an alcove. Their round table was covered with a white linen cloth, and red candles flickered in brass candlesticks. Piano music sounded softly in the background.

Grady reached below the table and gave Clarice's hand a squeeze, and she squeezed back. She looked around the group. Theo's mass of brown curls and pink cheeks contrasted with his staid charcoal suit. He was seated between Kent and Harriet O'Toole, and he seemed to be entertaining Harriet with one of his stories. Kent had combed his hair in a new style, with a part down the center, and he was dressed in an uncustomary white shirt and dark slacks.

Clarice's gaze continued around the table to her father, who was sipping a glass of wine. His rimless glasses had slipped down his nose. His long thin face bore no resemblance to Theo's. With straight brown hair and pale skin, her father's only similarity to Uncle Theo was his blue eyes. She saw her father had on his nine-year-old tan suit, and as her gaze shifted to her mother, she knew her mother's dress was almost as old as her father's suit. She sighed, thinking how well-matched her parents were, as alike as two halves of the same leaf. Her mother was pretty, with big blue eyes behind gold-rimmed glasses. Her features were symmetrical and had been inherited by her son. Her hair was fastened in a bun at the back of her head and she wore no makeup. Clarice knew without question why she had grown up a little old-fashioned for the present day.

Over green salads served on chilled crystal plates, her father turned to Grady. "What line of work are you in?"

Clarice didn't know if she imagined it or not, but suddenly the music seemed softer and all attention seemed to be on Grady.

"He's an engineer," Harriet O'Toole said, and smiled.

"Is that right? What company are you with?"

Inwardly Clarice braced for what was coming next, listening to Grady answer, "Well, right now—"

"He has his own company, O'Toole Drilling,

Incorporated," his mother answered, and Grady smiled at her.

"That's not what—"

Grady broke off as the waiter appeared with their dinners, whisking away the salad plates and placing the varied entrees before each of the diners. Clarice looked down at her steamy golden chicken breast Marsala on a bed of brown rice with crisp green cuts of broccoli, but her thoughts weren't on the food. She was wondering how long before the subject of Grady's job would come up again. She didn't have to wonder long. Her father asked her uncle, "Are you enjoying work at King's Crown, Theo?"

"Oh, I'm no longer there. Stanton let me go."

"I didn't know that." Her father frowned. "What're you doing?"

Clarice closed her eyes as Theo answered, "I'm selling hot tamales."

"Oh, good Lord! That's no job. Have you thought about going back to the flower place?"

"No. I'm enjoying this. It's out in the sunshine and you meet nice people."

"Hot tamales!"

"I'm selling them, too, Dad," Kent said.

"For Lord's sake, Kent! Not you too!"

"I think I should mention that I'm out of engineering," Grady said firmly. "I'm in the hot-tamale business and you're talking to my two employees."

This time Grady's mother closed her eyes. Grady smiled at Clarice's parents, who were staring at him. Her father frowned. "You've gone from engineering to tamales?"

"Yes, sir. It's a change and I've rather enjoyed it."

"You're the fellow Stanton was—" Her father bit

off his sentence and Clarice could imagine the rest of it. Uncle Stanton had probably raged about Grady and the tamale stand sometime when he had talked to her father.

"Well, it's a temporary situation," Mrs. O'Toole said brightly.

"No, Mom, it might not be," Grady said with such cheer Clarice wanted to shake her fist at him.

"What're you talking about?" Mrs. O'Toole asked with a frown, and Clarice gave up hope of the conversation changing to a safer topic.

"I may stay in this whatever the outcome about the drilling company."

"Oh, Grady!" Mrs. O'Toole exclaimed in such tones of woe there was no question how she felt.

"It's really a charming job, Mrs. O'Toole," Uncle Theo said. "I've met the most interesting people. Aren't there people you've met who're unforgettable?"

"Well, yes."

"Who?" Uncle Theo asked with a smile.

She looked startled, but then she began to talk about someone she had met at Yellowstone Park, and while Theo listened attentively, Kent said, "Did you see the Cowboys win last Monday night, Dad?"

"That last touchdown was a dilly," her father said, and football became the topic of conversation among the men. Still, Clarice noticed the curious glances that her parents gave Grady throughout the rest of the meal.

After they had finished and taken everyone home, Grady drove Clarice to his condo. "I like your folks," he said quietly as he unlocked the door and pushed it open. One single light burned in the living room, spilling faint rays into the dusky hall. Grady loosened his tie and smiled at her, then closed and locked the door.

"I'm glad you liked them," she said. "I liked your mother. She's charming."

"She and Theo enjoyed each other immensely, I thought. Of course, Theo enjoys everyone." He put his arm around her and led her toward the kitchen. "Come in and I'll get us something cool to drink. I think you'll hear from your parents about dating a tamale vendor."

"I might. But they let me lead my own life pretty much."

"Mom's totally taken with you. She sees a girl after her own heart."

"What does that mean?"

He straightened up behind the open refrigerator door and smiled at her. "Sweetie, you're the kind of woman my mother would love."

"Grady, I'm beginning to feel a thousand years old and as square as your tamale cart."

His eyes sparkled and he shrugged. "If the shoe fits . . ." He took a cold beer and a bottle of pop out of the refrigerator, kicked the door shut, and turned his back as he fumbled in the drawer for an opener.

She walked up behind him, placing her hands on his thighs as she pressed against him, then stood on tiptoe and kissed the nape of his neck. "Square, huh?"

"I'm afraid so. Like my tamale cart," he said softly, his voice teasing. He turned his head slightly and she kissed his ear, moving her hips against him provocatively.

"Old-fashioned?" she whispered, her tongue

flicking out to touch his ear again while her hands slipped caressingly over his hips.

"As old-fashioned as hair ribbons and straw hats," he said, but his breathing had deepened and his voice had grown husky. She wiggled her hips against him, hearing him draw a sharp breath. He turned to wrap his arms around her.

"Lordy," he said. He gazed at her hungrily, his hands moving down over her buttocks to fit her closer against him while he lowered his head to kiss her. She trembled with eagerness and shoved aside differences and problems as she returned his kiss.

Their lovemaking was long and passionate, and Clarice's feelings were edged with a touch of desperation. She didn't want to lose Grady.

Eleven

Problems of another kind surfaced two days later when Uncle Stanton called Clarice into his office. "Eileen just quit," he said. "You can take her section of tables and work it in between seating customers."

"Yes, sir. What about my hours?"

"They're posted on the bulletin board in the kitchen." He took off his gray sharkskin jacket and rolled up his white shirt-sleeves. "We're getting rid of the tamale stand."

"You are?"

"Yep. Had to buy the man out, but that land will be clear and mine, and no tacky hot-tamale stand will mar the grounds around here. I hear you're dating him."

"Yes, I am," she said, mulling over the most important new development in her life. Grady was moving. No more tamale stand only yards away.

"You're wasting your time dating a fellow who's like a Gypsy. He and Theo are cut out of the same cloth."

"Maybe in some ways, but not in others. He's suing his cousin for the business they shared."

"You don't say. What kind of business?"

"A drilling company. Grady O'Toole is an engineer."

Uncle Stanton looked up from the papers on his desk. "The man's an engineer and he's out peddling tamales? He's a nut. A bonafide nut. Stay away from him, Clarice, if you want a bit of advice."

"I think Mom and Dad rather liked him."

"Yeah, well, I'm looking at him with a more practical approach. Man may be pleasant, but stay away from him. Security's important in life."

"Yes, sir."

"Close my door when you leave, will you?"

"Yes, sir," she said, and did as he asked. She went to the kitchen and felt a flash of anger when she saw the additional hours she would be working.

With her emotions in an upheaval she marched determinedly back to Uncle Stanton's office. She knocked on the door, then entered without waiting. Uncle Stanton frowned when he looked up.

"I just looked at my hours," she said. "Will I get paid overtime?"

" 'Course not. You're in management and you're on a salary."

"I'll be working eight hours more a week. Do you realize what my total weekly hours will be?"

"You want a career here? Listen, young lady, I worked eighty hours a week when I got started."

"You were the owner. I don't get a raise?"

"After a time if you're doing a good job. You've worked here just a little over two months now. No, you don't get a raise now. And I can't play favorites with relatives."

"Cuong got a raise recently."

"Cuong is my chef. He's vital to the restaurant and one of the finest chefs in the city. And he's worked here two years. He didn't get a raise after two months."

Uncle Stanton bent his head over the desk and Clarice knew she had been dismissed. She went back to work, but during a break in the afternoon she drove down the street to a pay phone. While traffic rushed past on the street she dialed Dr. McClellan's office and asked to speak to him. Ten minutes later she drove back to King's Crown to turn in her resignation.

She asked Uncle Stanton to step into his office and he sat behind his desk, his features impassive as she told him she was quitting.

"I'm returning to my old job at the dentist's office."

"Whatever you think you have to do," he said calmly, and she suddenly had a suspicion he might have wanted to get rid of her.

"I'll give you two weeks notice so you'll have time to hire someone."

"You don't need to, Clarice. Margo can fill in your job."

"At lower pay," she said, realizing he would be ahead either way. Margo at lower pay or Clarice at longer hours.

"She's not as experienced and she's not family."

Suppressing the anger she felt over his tactics, she asked, "How long do you need me to stay?"

"Suit yourself."

"Then I'll finish out the week."

"Fine, Clarice. Anytime you want to come back,

let me know. I'm sorry to see you go," he added, and she knew he was ready for her to leave his office so he could get back to his bookkeeping.

"Yes, sir." She left feeling angry and frustrated.

Her anger only increased that night when she faced Grady across a checkered tablecloth as they finished steak dinners. He leaned back, his white shirt contrasting with his dark skin as his eyes flashed with anger. "You just quit? You didn't protest?"

"No, it wouldn't have done a bit of good," she said, shifting in the chair, her navy cotton skirt falling in folds over her knees.

"You let him walk all over you. Theo did and Kent did."

"Whereas you go after your relatives with a sledgehammer."

His face flushed and they stared at each other. "Let's get on a safe subject," he said quietly.

"All right." She tried to acquiesce, but it was difficult. "What's safe?"

"When do you start at the dentist's?"

"Monday morning."

"Will you make the same salary you did at the restaurant?"

"No. I won't make as much. I don't think this is a safe subject, Grady. Maybe we don't have a safe subject."

His eyes darkened as if he'd received a blow, and his jaw firmed. After a pause he asked, "Have you heard about the man who stops every Wednesday to talk to Theo?"

"I don't think so. I've been too busy to see Uncle Theo since the night we were all together."

Grady smiled and Clarice wanted to fling herself

into his arms and forget all their disputes. He said, "There's a man who comes every Wednesday and he's been on one of the crews to hunt the Loch Ness monster. Needless to say, Theo is entranced."

She laughed. "You may lose your employee. It always amazed me that Uncle Theo never traveled, but since I've gotten older I've realized he gets his joy out of people, not places. He's happy right here because he can find an endless source of fascination in people. Grady, where are you moving to?" She had been waiting for him to tell her, but he hadn't mentioned it and she couldn't resist asking. "Uncle Stanton told me you sold your lot."

"I've leased another spot," he said, and went on to talk about an antique clock he'd just purchased and wanted to show her. She decided there must be some reason he was evading the subject of his new location, but she let it drop.

The tension between them eased a fraction until they were in his car. Grady seemed worried as he glanced at her and said flatly, "I'd like to show you something."

"Sure," she said, hating the wall going up between them. She reached over to hold his hand, and his fingers locked around hers. "I read in the paper about your suit."

"Yeah. I was hoping that wouldn't get in the news. We're trying to reach an agreement out of court. By the way, Mom wants you to come over again."

"Anytime," she said lightly. Grady swung into an empty parking lot in front of a string of red brick shops along the busy freeway. He stopped and helped her out of the car. With a questioning look she went with him as he crossed the walk to an empty glass-fronted space. Her reflection was a dim blur in the glass, the faint white of her blouse showing, a dark shadow reflecting her navy skirt as she waited while Grady fished a key out of his jeans pocket. He unlocked the door and looked down at her. "Your uncle Theo found this for me." He waved his arm and announced, "Step into O'Toole's tamales-to-be."

"This will be your restaurant?"

"Yes."

She entered the long, empty shop. One blue-white fluorescent light was on at the back. Amazed and puzzled, Clarice looked at the bare room, then she looked at Grady and saw he was waiting for her to say something.

"It's grand!"

"You really think so?"

"Yes. This is why you wouldn't talk about selling your lot to Uncle Stanton."

"Right. I wanted to surprise you."

"It's super, but where's the kitchen?"

"I'm having it redone. They start tomorrow. Want to help decorate it?" He asked her casually, but she felt an undercurrent, as if it were of monumental importance to him.

"I'd love to! This isn't what I expected. It's really great."

He smiled and she could see he was pleased. He took her arm. "C'mere," he urged, his voice changing from flat, wary tones to excitement. "Right here is where I'm putting the partition for the kitchen, and it'll be low, a counter with a cash register. I want customers to be able to see the kitchen and watch us making tamales. There should be room out here for about nine tables."

She stared at the rectangular room. "You could have booths put along that wall and use about seven tables and get more in that way," she said.

"Hey! You're right." He hugged her. "I knew I brought you here for some reason."

She looked up and smiled. He kissed her lightly, then his attention returned to the shop. "Which sounds best, O'Toole's Tamales or O'Toole's Tamale Café?"

"I still like O'Toole's Tamales. This is much more . . . than what I thought you'd have. You talked about a shoestring."

"Well, I need a good location. I'd be pouring money down a rathole if I were in an obscure spot where no one could find me."

"Doesn't this cost a lot?"

"I'm putting all my savings into getting this going," he said, suddenly solemn.

"Oh, Grady! What a risk!"

"I think I can make a go of it."

"But what if you don't? Grady, it's terrifying to think what you're risking! Time and money, the savings you've put away over the years. And all for tamales?"

"They're selling well. I've got a product people like. I don't intend to stand out on a street corner the rest of my life. We're in agreement on that much!"

"How can you risk your future when you don't have to? It isn't as if you don't have a choice," she said, hurting for him, wishing he would look at all aspects of what he was doing.

"I see a chance here, just as I did when I started the drilling company."

"This is entirely different!"

His eyes narrowed and the harshness came back into his voice. "I think we're on dangerous ground again. Let's go."

In the car he was silent, and she felt a chasm opening between them, one she was helpless to stop because it was so basic. As they walked to the door of her apartment, she grasped his hand. "What's happening to us, Grady?"

"I guess you'd call it a difference in temperament." He said coldly, and it hurt.

At the door she turned to look at him, slipping her hands up his arms. He held her lightly, looking at her in the intense way she had seen him do more and more lately. Suddenly he pulled her into his arms and kissed her hard. She clung to him until he released her abruptly. "I'll call," he said, and walked down the steps. She had a feeling their parting was final.

As the days passed she saw she was right. Grady didn't call and she knew they had reached an impasse in their views. She went to work at her old job and tried to get over Grady. As time passed she found it more difficult instead of less to forget him. She missed him and she felt incomplete. And to her amazement, she wasn't happy in the old routine of answering the phone and typing dental bills and keeping the appointment ledger. She was bored. She missed the work at King's Crown, and she began to look back over her life and ahead. Ahead looked terribly empty.

Finally she sat down to rethink how she viewed her life. And gradually, little by little, she began to change.

The last part of September came, and during a long tedious afternoon when there were few patients and little to do, she spent the hours thinking about her future and about Grady. She closed up and drove purposefully to King's Crown. As she turned in the drive she saw the tamale stand was gone. She felt a pang, remembering Grady's dancing eyes, his marvelous chest. She firmed her lips, brushing her hand over her tan skirt, and marched into the restaurant.

Uncle Stanton, dressed in his usual gray sharkskin slacks, was in the kitchen talking to Cuong. Both of them greeted Clarice, Cuong's dark eyes lighting with pleasure. They chatted a moment before she asked, "Uncle Stanton, may I see you please?"

"Of course. I'll be back, Cuong, and we'll finish going over the menu for the Sunday brunch." He led the way to his office and sat down behind the desk to face her. "Have a chair, Clarice."

"Thank you."

"How's the dental office?"

"It's a little dull after working here."

"Oh? You want your old job back?"

"No, I don't, but I want to tell you, I don't think you were fair to Uncle Theo, Kent, or me. You made promises to us and you didn't keep them. That isn't right, relatives or not. An agreement is an agreement."

He looked startled, then he frowned. "Well, Clarice, I have to keep things going here and I can't be extravagant—"